Quest

By

Nate Johnson

Purple Herb Publishing

AuthorNateJo@gmail.com

https://www.facebook.com/AuthorNateJo/

Dedicated to
Cade Goodman
A young man to be proud of

Other books by Nate Johnson

Quest

Chapter One

Cassie

Believe me. I knew life could be unfair. I was a sixteen-year-old girl with a dead mother. But even I didn't expect the universe to be so cruel.

I was mucking out the stalls with my best friend Sara Thompson when I got the call.

"Hey Dad," I said as I answered. "It's only been two days, checking up on me already?"

"Blue Jester," he said and my heart dropped. That was the family code word. Shut up, this was serious. No joking.

"Yes sir," I said as I looked at Sara. I could see that she saw the sudden fear in my eyes.

"Listen, Honey," he said, "The asteroid is going to hit. They made a mistake."

I gulped then said, "Are you sure?"

He scoffed, "It's math. Of course I'm sure. It's going to hit in the Pacific ..."

"Ryan?" I gasped, our home was a mile from the beach in Seattle. My dad was an astrophysicist. A professor. I'd grown up with stories about asteroids and the damage they could do.

"I just talked to him. He'd headed to Papa's in Idaho. I've talked to Haley in New York, and Chase in the Sierras. I've told them to get to Papa's place."

"Should I go there?" I asked as I held my breath. How was I supposed to get to Idaho from Oklahoma?

"NO," he barked. "It is too dangerous. The Thompsons will take care of you."

My stomach clenched. "For how long? I mean, are you coming here?" God, I wanted my dad more than anything in the world.

There was a long pause on the other end. So long I wondered if the connection had been broken.

"No," he said with a sadness in his voice that shredded my insides. "This is going to be bad. A dinosaur killer type bad. You stay there. If you can't stay. If things ... if you have to leave then you and the Thompsons try for your grandfather's."

"Dad, that's over a thousand miles away. And if there's an EMP cars won't work.

"That's why I'm telling you to stay there."

My mind fought to understand. My family was spread out across the country. Dad was in California, Ryan in Washington.

Haley in New York. And Chase, who knew? This wasn't right. The world couldn't end. I hadn't finished High School.

"How long? Until," I asked.

"Ten minutes. You guys will be okay there. It's probably the best spot in the world."

"Minutes," I gasped. "You're still at JPL, aren't you? That's like ten miles from the beach."

"Don't worry about me," he said as my heart broke into a thousand pieces. I could hear it in his voice. He didn't expect to survive this. I mean, my dad, the strongest man I would ever know. He'd survived the death of his wife and brother, raised his two children, and taken on my two cousins. He'd borne the weight of the world. And been the best dad ever. Always supporting us. Pushing us to do better without being overbearing.

Swallowing hard, I tried to hold back the tears but they came anyway. "I love you, Dad."

He sniffled on the other end then said, "I will always love you, Cassie. You are special. I am so proud of you. Your mother would have been also."

My heart broke as I fought to figure out what to say next. How could I let him know how important he was?

"I've got to go," he said suddenly. "There may be a way out for me. I love ..."

I gasped as the line went dead, his voice cut off. I wondered if I would ever talk to my father again. My heart broke as I struggled to make sense of everything.

"What?" Sara asked as she stared at me.

"The world is ending," I told her as I stared at the phone in my hand. "My Dad. He says the asteroid is going to hit. The one in the news. And it's big."

"They said it would miss us by a ton of miles," Sara replied.

Shrugging, I said, "They were wrong."

"Are you sure?" she asked, obviously unable to believe it.

"My dad is, that means it is going to happen. He is never wrong. Not about stuff like this."

The two of us stood there staring at each other, both unable to process what was going on. I will never forget that moment when I realized that my world was literally going to come to an end.

I still remember the smell of the barn. Brandy, Sara's horse sticking his head out the stall door and raising an eyebrow. The chickens scratching through the hay, waiting for us to clear her mother's horse, Cimarron's, stall.

But it is that gut-sick feeling I will never forget. It was the same feeling I had when I learned my mom had been killed by a drunk driver. As if I'd been dropped into a bottomless pit. Always falling. No sense of solid under my feet. A gut-wrenching fear. My father? My brother? My cousins? Had I lost them all?

"We should call my Mom," Sara said as she pulled out her phone.

"Call Mom why?" A male voice asked from behind us.

I turned to find Sara's older brother Luke staring at us, his Australian cattle dog, Clancy, next to him. Short-haired, gray, with patches of black and brown. Luke shook his head. "They went into town grocery shopping. Leave them alone. It's there only time together all week."

Sara glared at her brother. "Cassie's dad just called. He said the asteroid is going to hit us."

I've got to give him credit. He didn't scoff or roll his eyes at his crazy sister. But then Luke Thompson was too cool to ever show that much emotion. The boy was all lanky cowboy. Tall, wide at the shoulder, and narrow at the hip. And he continually pissed me off to no end.

9

Sara and I had been best friends for ten years. Since the first day of first grade. And I swear he hadn't said ten words to me in those ten years. And three of those had been, pass the salt.

I'm sure when I moved away last summer he hadn't even noticed.

"My dad said," I began, "That it is going to hit in the Pacific, in the next few minutes. It is big. As big as the one that killed the dinosaurs."

He frowned as he looked down at the cast on his wrist. Sara hadn't told me how yet. But it was probably doing something pretty cool.

"You better call Mom," he said. "She'd be pissed if we didn't."

Sara punched at her phone then began to pace as she waited for her mom to pick up. Next, she got ready to send a text. Suddenly she froze then looked down at her phone as the color drained from her face. "it's dead. It was working, now nothing."

Luke scowled as he shook his head then snatched the phone out of his sister's hands. Holding it up, he twisted, obviously trying to catch a better signal but he stopped and stared at the phone then said to me, "Is yours working."

I pulled mine out and felt my stomach drop, nothing. No power, no bars. Suddenly I felt a cold shiver shoot down my spine. "No," I managed to say, unable to look away from the phone in my hand.

Luke continued to frown. Sara tried to reach for her phone but he pulled away and marched outside, holding the phone up, twisting again.

"There's no power," I said as we followed him outside. "It isn't the signal."

He continued to twist then suddenly froze and stared up into the sky. All three of us stood there, frozen, as we watched an airliner fall out of the sky. It came down at a steep angle. Not a glide.

I held my breath, praying it would pull out. But instead, it disappeared beyond the horizon. A moment later, a black cloud rose from where the plane had disappeared followed by the distant roar of an explosion.

"What is going on?" Luke mumbled under his breath.

I couldn't stop thinking about those people in the plane. Plummeting to their deaths. Knowing they were going to die and being unable to do anything to stop it. Mothers sitting with their children. Young couples leaving for their honeymoon. Businessmen returning home. Their families would be waiting for them at the airport. Only to never see them again.

A numbness washed over me. Everything was happening too fast. I couldn't deal with it all.

"Here," Luke snapped as he handed the dead phone back to Sara then stomped off back to the house.

The Thompson's farm was a hundred and sixty acres. They'd kept forty for themselves and rented out the rest to a local farmer. The distant fields were scattered with corn stubble waiting for spring planting.

Lost. I was completely lost. My foundation had crumbled. I will admit that a small part of me was self-centered enough to want to whine. I'd been pulled away from my friends and forced to move across the country in the middle of high school. My mother died when I was ten. My family was scattered across the country during the worst natural disaster imaginable.

I took a deep breath as I glanced over at Sara. The confusion in her eyes let me know she was feeling the same way. Nothing made sense anymore.

Suddenly she yelled, "Luke," and hurried after him.

I followed because what else was I going to do?

She caught up to her brother and pulled at his arm to stop him. "What are we supposed to do?"

He frowned down at her and said, "How should I know?"

Sara blanched as the color drained from her face. This was her older brother Luke. He always knew what to do in any situation. Heaven knows he told her often enough.

Taking a deep breath, he glanced at me, then again at his sister before sighing heavily. "Let's try the landline in the house."

Sara suddenly perked up.

The three of us hurried into the house only to find it dark. The silence was ear-shattering. No air conditioner. No refrigerator hum. Nothing but the click of Clancy's toe nails on the linoleum.

The three of us looked at each other, mirroring the fear in each other's eyes.

The old fashioned yellow phone hung on the wall in the kitchen. Sara had told me that her mom had said back in the old days it had been the only phone in the house and if she wanted to talk to her boyfriend she had to do it in front of her dad.

Sara had shuddered at the thought. But it sort of worked out because her mom ended up marrying that boyfriend. But still. Can you imagine such ancient technology? One phone. In the middle of the house?

Luke picked up the receiver and frowned as he held it to his ear. Holding it out he said, "No dial tone."

"What is going on," Sara asked.

"An EMP," I said. "The Asteroid is made out of metal. When it hits the atmosphere it creates an EMP."

"What's that?" Sara asked.

Luke continued to scowl.

"Electrical Magnetic Pulse," I said as if that answered everything. "It knocks out electronics. Transformers, computer chips, stuff like that."

"Airplanes?" Luke asked.

"Yes," I told him. "Dad used to talk about it happening.

"How long will it be out?" he asked me. "The Electricity."

I took a deep breath before I said, "Forever."

Chapter Two

Luke

It was impossible to believe. But a plane falling out of the sky sort of made it real. No power, no phones, those I could understand. But planes crashing. All at the same time. Cassie's dad's warning had been real.

Face it, the world was ending. I couldn't pretend it wasn't

I stared at the dead phone on the wall and tried to think what to do. Mom and Dad, obviously. They were in town. Ten miles away. Without saying anything I stormed back outside to my old F-150 pickup and slid in over the ancient leather seat. When I turned the key I got nothing. Not even a click.

Looking up, both girls stood on the porch staring at me. Okay, this EMP crap was getting serious. I had never been into that Sci-Fi stuff. If I couldn't do it from the back of a horse then I wasn't interested. But it seemed Cassie had been right. Nothing worked.

What did that mean?

I sat in my truck and stared at the two girls. My gut tightened as I realized I didn't have a clue on what to do next. Go into town and find Mom and Dad? Wait? And both of the girls were looking at me like I had some kind of clue.

Slamming the truck door closed I stomped back into the house. "Tell me about this EMP stuff," I said to Cassie.

She frowned then shrugged. "My brother and Dad used to talk about it. Basically, it is some kind of electrical explosion that burns out chips. Anything with a computer gets fried unless it is protected. Switches. Anything with a small gap that a spark can burn through."

I glanced out the window to my truck and cursed under my breath. The truck was ancient, eighteen years old. But it still had a chip running things. You'd have to go back to the seventies to find something that didn't.

"Let me guess," I said. "There's no fixing the chip. They've got to be replaced."

She scoffed as she nodded. "And the computer chip place isn't going to work anymore. So don't hold your breath."

Taking a deep breath I let it out slow then looked around. "Okay Sara," I said to my sister. "Break out the storm lanterns. We'll need them tonight."

"We were going riding," my sister said with that pout of hers that pisses me off.

"Tough," I snapped. "Mom and Dad are going to want you here when they get back."

She sighed heavily then nodded.

"You guys can finish cleaning the barn," I told them. " I'll be out there to help in a bit. Just get the lamps before it gets dark."

Both girls stared back at me like I'd become their worst nightmare. "What?" I asked.

"You're not in charge of me. Or Cassie," Sara said as she put her hands on her hips and gave me the stink eye.

I studied her for a long moment then laughed. Which made her cheeks glow red with pure anger. "Fine," I said, "sit here in a hot house and do what ever you want. Just don't leave the farm."

Both girls stared back at me then Cassie grabbed my sister's hand and nodded to the barn. The girl wasn't an idiot. She knew it was better to keep busy.

Sara shot me an angry glare and then followed her friend out.

Now what? I wondered as I looked around the house. The uncertainty ate at my gut. This was all new. I'd rather be riding an angry bull than deal with the unknown. At least with a bull I had experienced the worst they could do. This stuff was too freaking weird how was I supposed to know what to expect.

Sighing, I glanced over at the cupboards in the kitchen. We were okay for food. Mom and Dad would be returning with a bunch more food. Plus the chickens and eggs. Suddenly it hit me. Rushing over I tried the faucet and received nothing but a sputtering and spit. Then nothing.

The well was down. No power, no well, no water. The animals should be okay for a couple of days. Both troughs in the fields were full and the one in the coral was almost full. Suddenly I remembered and smiled to myself.

My grandfather had shown me one time. We'd been in his tool shed. A hodge podge of spare parts and his work bench. On a shelf buried behind some ancient mouse traps, he'd shown me the hand pump for the well. He'd shaken his head and told me about how when his father had been my age he'd had to pump water every morning for his mom. And how they'd used an outhouse.

I swear he'd sounded proud about how rough it had been. But I was eight years old and just thought it was stupid to not have electricity.

Laughing to myself, I shook my head. Something told me that grandfather would be laughing his butt off at me.

Still shaking my head I tapped my leg for Clancy to follow then went out to the tool room. It took me half the morning rutting around before I found the ancient hand pump. It took me another hour to pull the pump up out of the well then attach the hand pump.

The cast on my wrist didn't make it easy.

I had to empty the coral trough to prime the pump. Then pump out a dozen buckets of water to refill the trough once I had everything going.

Standing back I smiled to myself as I removed my hat and wiped my brow. I'd at least accomplished one thing today. Would Dad think it was the right thing to focus on? What if the power came back? We'd have a useless pump and forty feet of hose sitting in the tool shed.

When I got back to the house I found Sara standing in front of the refrigerator with both doors open, staring at the contents.

"You're letting the cold air out," I told her.

She glared at me then said, "We're going to have to cook everything before it spoils."

"No. We'll wait for Mom and Dad."

Rolling her eyes she slammed the doors closed and stormed off to her room.

I glanced over at Cassie who shook her head and said, "You're a jerk."

"What'd I do?" I asked, completely confused. And what gave this little girl the right to call me a jerk?

She just shook her head and followed my sister into her room.

I stared at their door and tried to understand what I had done that was so terrible. And since when did Cassie Conrad think I was a jerk? I mean she barely knew me. We hadn't shared a dozen words in the ten years she'd been hanging around Sara.

God, the last thing I needed was another crazy girl around here. My sister was crazy enough.

I ended up wrapping some diced potatoes in foil and cooking three steaks over the Bar-B-Q. When I called the girls for dinner they both shot me angry stares. I ignored them and asked, "Did you break out the storm lanterns."

Sara sighed heavily then said, "You said before dark. It isn't dark yet."

I wanted to snap at her but bit my tongue and let out a long slow breath before focusing on my dinner.

After finishing, I decided to make a round before it got too dark to see. I checked the front gate and stood there for a moment looking up the road. Mom and Dad would have to walk home. Ten, Eleven miles. They should have been here by now. They'd had all day.

My gut clinched up tighter than a preacher's wallet, as my grandfather would have said. Where were they? I mean this was the end of the world. They should be here, with us.

I gave the road one long last look then sighed heavily and turned to leave. I confirmed the chickens were closed up for the night. All four horses were in the corral with access to alfalfa and water. Clancy snuck under the bottom rail and made a tour of the corral to make sure everything was still alright.

The horses ignored the dog. They'd spent too many hours together. That was why I'd gotten him two years ago. He could keep up with them for days.

Reaching over the fence I scratched Ajax's forehead and patted his neck. He nudged my hand looking for a carrot or apple.

"Not tonight," I told him then confirmed the gate was locked before leaving him. You lucky bastards, I thought to myself. The horses had no idea how things had changed. To them, there was no difference. They had water, they had food. To them, their world was working.

Before going back to the house I stopped at the tool room and used a pair of tin snips to cut off my cast. I'd hated the thing for the last six weeks. But I was pretty sure I wasn't going to be going to a doctor's to get it cut off. So I might as well do it now.

The hand and wrist were pale and itched like no tomorrow.

When I got back to the house I saw that Sara had broken out the storm lanterns and had two of them working.

"Your cast?" Cassie asked with a deep frown.

I shrugged then took one of the lamps out onto the porch where I could keep an eye on the road for when Mom and Dad got back. They'd want a light to show them the way.

"How did you break your wrist?" Cassie asked as both girls came out to join me on the porch.

I felt my cheeks grow warm.

"A bull stomped on it," Sara said and I swear there was a hint of pleasure in her voice. I didn't know if it was because I had been hurt, or because she knew I didn't like talking about it.

"His first bull ride in the adult category and he's thrown in three seconds. Lands under the bull and gets his wrist stomped on. Two bones broken."

"Jesus," I snapped. "Don't sound so pleased."

She frowned then shrugged. "I'm not glad you got hurt. Just glad you weren't perfect. I get tired of you being perfect all the time."

I stared at her unable to understand then looked over at Cassie as if she could explain it. Seeing I wouldn't get any help there. I reached down and scratched Clancy's head and focused on the road.

The moon dipped out from behind a cloud and I began to realize just how late it had gotten. Where were Mom and Dad? I think it was at that moment were I started to really worry. What if something had happened? What if we had to go through the end of the world without them?

Chapter Three

Cassie

My stomach refused to settle. I was being bombarded by a thousand worries and the occasional terrifying thought. My family? The Thompsons? Would they let me stay with them? I mean. I was a guest. But what if they didn't want me? I'd have to walk to Idaho.

The thought sent a cold shiver down my back.

And where were Sara's parents? Suddenly, the thought of being around adults didn't sound so terrible. Yesterday at this time if you'd told me I was craving parental oversight I'd have laughed in your face. Now, I'd give anything to have my dad walking down the driveway to us. His big smile letting me know everything was all right.

Where was he? I wondered. The asteroid had hit us twelve hours ago. Had he gotten away? Please, I begged. I couldn't lose another parent.

And Ryan. My big brother. Had he gotten out of Seattle in time? Would I ever know what happened to them?

Except for the effects of the EMP, we wouldn't have any clue that something terrible had happened. No flash in the sky. No roaring boom. Just another pretty spring day outside of Tulsa Oklahoma.

I glanced over at Sara and sighed. The three of us were sitting on the porch waiting for Sara's parents. The lightning bugs were coming out, sparking in the dark as the occasional mosquito buzzed around looking for a place to land.

Luke slapped his neck and shook his head. He got up then came back with a citronella candle, lit it, and put it on the table to keep the bugs away.

"Where are they?" Sara asked.

Luke shrugged. "It's a long walk. And knowing dad, he's trying to figure out a way to get all the groceries back. He'd never abandon them. Not after he'd paid for them."

Sara frowned then asked, "What is going to happen?"

Both of them looked at me like I had some kind of idea. That is what happens when you live with a famous scientist, people think you know things. If it had been a question about horses, or ranching, they'd have been able to explain in deep detail. But space stuff was in my world. Or at least my dad's.

"It depends," I said then saw that my answer wasn't going to be enough. "It depends on the size, angle, and where it hits." I was pulling up old dinner table conversations. "The dinosaur killer asteroid didn't kill them all at once. Not all of them. It took hundreds of years. The climate changed, dust in the air. And even then, they evolved into birds."

Luke's frown deepened. "So you're saying people are going to die out in the next hundred years?"

"Not all of them," I assured him.

"Not all of them!" Sara gasped. "How many is not all?"

I swallowed hard then said, "Most. I mean most will die. If not today, then over the next year. At least, that is what my dad used to say."

Both of their jaws dropped as they stared at me.

Taking a deep breath I continued, "The hit in the ocean will generate a huge tidal wave. That will kill a lot. Millions, Maybe more."

"More than millions, is a billion," Luke snapped, obviously unable to believe what he was hearing.

I nodded. "That is the first day. The EMP has knocked out electricity. So no transportation. No farming. Nothing moves. You can't get food to people. Not in the cities. More will die in the next six months. Then still more next year when we can't grow enough food. And more over the next decades as dust up in the high atmosphere blocks the sun so plants don't grow as well."

Luke twisted to stare out into the dark. He grunted as if he'd been punched in the gut then closed his eyes as he took a deep breath. Suddenly getting up, he stormed into the house then returned a minute later with a rifle.

"That's Dad's," Sara exclaimed.

Luke just nodded then sat backdown and looked over at me. "What else."

I shrugged. "How should I know? It's the end of the world as we knew it. Figure everything has changed."

A heavy silence fell over us as we each let our imaginations run wild.

"School?" Sara asked.

I shook my head as a sadness filled me. School, even up in Seattle was my place. I had made friends. And believe it or not. I liked it. Now it was gone. Along with Seattle now that I thought about it.

Luke let out a long breath then said, "Man, you're a fun person."

"Hey," I snapped. "You asked. If you don't want to know. Then don't ask."

He held up his hands and almost smiled. "I was only kidding. Jesus, calm down."

"Calm down," I growled. "I'm stuck a thousand miles away from my family. They might all be dead already. Calm down?" I bit down on my back teeth to stop from going off on him.

He frowned at me for a minute then nodded as if he almost agreed with me.

Again that awkward silence fell over us. The crickets chirped, emphasizing the silence. A warm wind came in from the south to ruffle the grass. I could hear the horses in the corral moving around, not skittish, just changing positions to catch the new wind.

Luke was staring into the darkness. Sara frowned down at her hands, both of them lost in their own world. Finally, Luke rubbed his recently freed wrist then said, "You guys should probably get some sleep. I'll wake you when Mom and Dad get here."

"What are you going to do?" Sara asked.

Luke shrugged then scooted his chair so that he could lean his head against the house and I knew he'd spend the night out here until his parents got home.

"Come on," I told Sara. "He's right. We can't do anything until they get here. Staying up and worrying won't help them get here any faster. And they are going to need our help tomorrow."

Sara frowned, but she finally nodded. We'd set up sleeping bags in her room for a week-long sleep over just like we used to do before I moved away last summer. God, I'd so looked forward to this time together for the last nine months. And now it was all ruined. There'd be no late-night giggling together. No make overs. No long rides on our horses. No talk about boys and our future.

No, everything had narrowed down to worrying about what was going to happen tomorrow. Not next week in school. Not two years from now and college. No, tomorrow, that was all that mattered.

I woke the next morning when a sunbeam poked around a window blind. Sara was curled up on her bed. Some time in the night she'd abandoned her bag for her bed. I guess we were done with the whole special bonding time during the sleep over.

My stomach clenched as I hurried up and out to the porch to find Luke in his chair, his arms across his chest.

"Your Mom and Dad?"

He grimaced then shook his head.

I fell into the chair next to him. I hadn't expected this. I'd expected them back long ago.

"I'm going into town," he said. "To see if they need help."

"We'll all go," I told him. "We'll take all four horses. I'll double up on Brandy with Sara for the ride back."

He thought for a moment then shook his head. "We don't know what we'll find along the way."

I buried the anger inside of me. I hated being told no. I stared at him then said, "Will we be safer here without you? You'd better leave us guns. And handling four horses isn't easy."

His eyes narrowed as he searched for a reason to dismiss me but finally, he nodded. "You better wake Sara. We need to get going.

We had a quick breakfast of untoasted pop tarts then saddled up. Me on Cimarron, Sara on her horse Brandy. Luke on his horse Ajax leading their dad's horse Cochise. I had to smile to myself. His dad had been a champion roper up until about ten years ago. He'd been offered big money for Cochise but turned it down saying he owed the horse a good life.

When we started, Luke's dog fell into step with us but Luke told him to stay and guard the place. The dog had looked up at his master and whined, obviously hating the idea of being left behind.

Luke ignored his pleas knowing he would do what he was told.

Initially, we road along the side of the road in the gravel until we came across a white SUV stopped in the middle of the road. It was then we realized there would be no traffic. There would be no one honking at us. Or whooshing by at a thousand miles an hour. I think that was the moment when I began to realize just how much things had changed. I'd known. But not known. Do you understand?

We passed the Thompson's neighbor, Mr. Sorrel, He had most of the land on the other side of the road. His big tractor was sitting in the middle of the field with the harrow behind it where he'd been prepping is fields for the spring planting.

I glanced over at Luke and saw the shock in his eyes. There would be no planting. No food grown.

On our side of the road were the Jensens. They farmed almost a thousand acres, including the land they rented from the Thompsons.

A mile later we passed two cars wrapped around each other at an intersection. I looked both ways and could see no cars for a mile in any direction.

Sara shook her head. "What are the chances both of them were at this spot when the EMP hit? They lost control and hit each other. A second either way and they wouldn't have been close.

Luke swung down from his horse and handed the reins to me so that he could look in the cars and make sure no one was hurt inside.

"It's clear," he said as he took the reins back and climbed back up into the saddle.

We continued through the countryside. Passing farms. Occasionally we would see people. A woman in a cotton dress on her porch waved. A man coming out of his barn stared at us until he identified the Thompson kids then relaxed. Cattle in fields.

The countryside was a mix. Flat. Fields, either corn or open prairie grass for cattle. Interspersed between sections of trees, mostly pine, and oak. But like I said. Flat. The Arkansas river was to our north about a mile. Tulsa was twenty miles to the east. Dad had taught there for years. I'd been born in the hospital. Mom was buried in Rose Hill cemetery.

But we'd hit the small town of Cleveland before we hit Tulsa. A small bedroom community. It had a Win-Co which was where Sara's mom and dad had gone shopping. Luke had said we'd start there.

As we drew closer to town, we noticed more cars stopped in the middle of the road.

34

Some had coasted to the side, but they'd all been abandoned. What else could people do? Sit in their car forever?

We stopped at a creek to water the horses then splashed across and back up onto the road. As we drew closer, I became nervous as I began to realize just how not right it had been for the Thompson's not to come home. What could have stopped them? I knew Mrs. Thomspon. Nothing would keep her from her children. She'd go mamma bear and tear anything apart that got in her way.

Mr. Thompson was steadier. But I'd seen him kill a rattle snake with a long stick like he was taking out the trash. Things didn't scare him.

When we hit town, we had to leave the gravel and ride down the middle of the road. I swear it was almost like we were in the July forth parade. People looked at us. But there was no smiling. No flags waving.

But it was the silence that hit me like running into a wall. Nothing. No car sounds. No air conditioners running in the distance. Nothing but the occasional soft word spoken by someone worried about disturbing this new silence.

As we got further into town, I noticed a thin column of smoke rising from ahead of us. It looked weird, not chimney smoke. To frazzled with hints of white mixed in with the sooty black.

My stomach clenched as a fear filled me.

We crested a small rise in the road and all three of us froze, halting our horses to stare at the destruction in front of us.

The Win-Co was a charred hole in the ground. A section of airplane tail sat in the middle of the parking long. Black smoke rose from smoldering humps of debris that used to be a grocery store. We sat there staring, unable to believe what we were seeing.

Then Luke cringed as he pointed. I followed his finger and saw his parents' truck sitting empty. Obviously, they had been inside when the plane fell out of the sky. Had they ever known they were in danger?

God, I hoped it had been fast.

Chapter Four

Luke

My mind refused to work as I stared ahead. What did it mean? It was impossible. No, this couldn't be happening. No way were my parents in that conflagration. No, No, a thousand times no.

Sara moaned deep in her throat as she was rocked with pure terror. "Luke?" she whispered.

Ajax shifted under me, obviously not liking the smell of smoke and charred debris. I instinctively squeezed with my knees to calm him down then looked again to confirm it was my dad's truck. The dent in the front bumper confirmed it. I'd made that dent four years earlier when I'd put it in the wrong gear and hit the fence post. Hey, I'd been fourteen and thought I knew what I was doing.

Dad had teased me about it for years. His way of keeping me humble, he had told me.

Had? Would he ever tease me again? NO. This was impossible. My mind whirled as I tried to understand.

The ground was black with twisted metal. A partial wall of cinder blocks marked the boundary of the former building.

Powdery black soot was littered with melted globs of material littering the blackened ruin.

No bodies. The fire must have been too intense.

"The Hospital," Sara gasped. "Maybe they took them to the hospital."

I clung to that idea, hoping for anything that might be a way out of this terror.

"We should go check," Cassie said as she leaned over to rest a hand on Sara's shoulder. The look in her eyes told me that she knew what my sister was going through. She'd lost her own mother, of course, she understood.

That thought filled me with anger. I hadn't lost my parents. How could I possibly think like that? No way. No, they were at the hospital. That was why they hadn't come home. Maybe only one was injured and the other had stayed with them.

Yes, that was it.

I gave Dad's truck one last look then pulled Ajax around to head for the hospital. Both girls fell in behind me. Sara was quiet, her eyes had a faraway look, and I worried about her going into shock.

Cassie shot me a quick look then back at her best friend.

It really wasn't much of a hospital. More of a clinic. Six weeks earlier I'd had my wrist wrapped in a cast in this very hospital. It had two rooms in the back to keep people overnight. Anything longer and they sent them to Tulsa.

Had my parents been sent to Tulsa? How? There were no ambulances. No rescue trucks. No, they would be at the clinic.

When we turned the corner onto the clinic's street, I pulled back on the reins to halt Ajax. The place was packed with a long line out front. Mostly old people, everyone with faraway stares. Some were sitting on the curb waiting their turn.

I swung down and handed Cassie the reins for Ajax and Cochise. Sara got down and joined me. "Do we get in line?" she asked.

The thought of waiting hours to find out if my parents were alive or not was not going to happen. "We're not here to get treated," I said and marched to the head of the line. Sara hurried to join me.

As we got there, I noticed an older nurse moving from person to person. Dressed in purple scrubs she had salt and pepper hair cut short and looked like she'd seen every emergency ever invented.

"Excuse me," I said as I interrupted her shining a light in an old man's eyes.

She ignored me as she finished her examination then patted the man on his shoulder while giving him a caring smile. Letting out a long breath, she turned back to me.

My stomach clenched as I got ready to ask the question. A fear filled me, yelling that I do not ask it. I didn't want to know. "The people, from the Win-Co, the airplane. Did they take them to Tulsa? Or are they here, inside?"

She looked up at me then over at Sara and frowned, "Oh honey, there were no survivors from the Win-co. I'm sorry."

My world dropped out from beneath me. Sara threw herself at my chest and started crying. That heavy ugly crying that might never stop. My arm went around her, holding her against my chest as I fought to understand. My parents couldn't be dead. This was impossible. No, I refused to believe it.

But deep inside. For the first time. A hint of doubt threatened to betray me. Too many things told me they weren't alive. They hadn't come home. Dad's truck was sitting there in the parking lot. Where were they?

The nurse moved on to check the next patient. Silently dismissing us. We weren't her problem. She had more than enough problems.

I pulled Sara away as I tried to figure out what to do next. A numbness washed over me. There would be no funeral. No chance to say goodbye. No closure.

My insides tightened as I began to realize just how much my world had changed. I mean no power, no electricity, planes falling out of the sky. No internet, No nothing. None of that mattered. It all paled compared to no parents.

In a cold fog, I watched as Sara climbed up on her horse and dropped her head, still crying, all while I tried to understand what to do next.

"We need to get back to take care of the animals," Cassie said softly, giving me focus. Giving me a reason to move.

I nodded as I took the reins back and swung up.

The ride back was one of the hardest things I had ever done in my life. I felt like I was abandoning them. There was nothing I could do. No decisions to make. I couldn't even dig a grave.

Sara cried softly. Cassie had tears trickling down her cheek. But I felt nothing but a numb coldness. It still wasn't real.

When we reached home, Cassie offered to put the horses away. Clancy looked at us and whined in the back of his throat as he glanced at the empty saddle on Cochise. He gave me a look, silently chastising me for leaving the pack leaders behind.

I wrapped my arm around Sara and led her to the house and into her room. I got her onto her bed then stopped at the door and looked back at my sister. She was devastated and I couldn't fix it for her. My heart broke. So many things were wrong. But my sister hurting like this was the worst of it.

I went back out onto the porch and stared across the fields, trying to understand.

After finishing watering and feeding the animals, Cassie went into the house and came back out with a glass of water and a peanut butter and jelly sandwich. Placing them both on the table next to my chair.

I glanced down at them then at her.

"You need to eat."

Scoffing, I shook my head.

Her brow furrowed. "You need to eat. Sara is … We, we are going to need you. This isn't like normal times."

Scoffing again, I said, "You think?"

She sighed heavily then rested a hand on my arm. "I know what you are going through."

"I know," I answered. I'd seen her when her mom had died. Sara had been her rock, helping her through it. Mom and Dad had bent over backward to make her feel part of our family. Letting her know she always had a place with us.

From what I had heard, her dad had stepped up, taken in the two cousins, and raised all four kids.

"But," she continued. "The world hadn't ended. It just felt like it. But not really. I had my Dad. My brother. Cousins. Society. Therapists. School, I had Sara, and your Mom. I had support."

Frowning, I glanced over at her trying to understand where this was going.

"You don't have all that. Not now."

An emptiness filled me as I realized just how right she was. There would be no social services to come check on us. No social security payments. No lawyers or cops. No funeral home. The world would continue to go on as if nothing had happened.

I couldn't even send word to my aunt in Austin. She would never know her brother had died when a plane fell out of the sky.

A sadness filled me as I began to accept it. My parents were dead. I couldn't deny it any longer. No begging would bring them back. An anger filled me as I realized I wouldn't have the time to grieve. That I would have to move on. Sara needed me.

Looking across at Cassie I nodded. "I'll be okay. I promise not to fall apart. You don't have to worry about me getting too emotional."

She frowned then shook her head. "Believe me, I would never worry about that. You are ... well never mind. I know you will keep it together."

I sighed then looked at the setting sun and said, "You know. There was this philosopher who once said, A man is judged by how he handles his father's death. Is he strong for the family? How is he at the funeral? We won't even have a funeral." I snapped as the anger came back in full force.

She squeezed my arm, holding it for a long minute then got up and said, "I need to check on Sara."

I nodded as she left me. Giving me space. Clancy rested his chin on my leg, wanting to be scratched. My fingers rubbed behind his ears as a new awareness hit me. I was in charge. I was responsible for keeping Sara and Cassie alive.

A cold fear filled me. I couldn't rely on Dad to make decisions. I would have to be the one. God, I wasn't ready for that weight. Especially not now. What if I screwed up? What if I got someone killed? No, I couldn't lose any more. Sara was all I had left in this world. The ranch, the horses, my future. None of it mattered compared to not losing Sara.

Slumping into my chair, I ground my teeth at the unrightness of it all. The unfairness. But it couldn't be ignored. Not if I was going to keep Sara and Cassie alive in this bad new world.

Deep in my gut, I knew things were not going to be easy. Of course, I never imagined just how bad they could get.

Chapter Five

Cassie

My heart broke when I looked in on Sara. Been there, done that, I thought. The ball of pain. Curled in on yourself crying so hard your stomach hurt and you relished the pain. Because you deserved it.

"Sara," I said as I sat on the bed next to her and put my hand on her back.

She continued to sob then slowly pulled herself back so she could speak between gasps of tears. "Do ... Do you think... still alive? Somewhere?"

I grimaced as I fought to figure out what to say. The truth? Or give her hope? But it would be false hope. If her parents were alive, they'd have been home already. Someone would have seen them.

Shaking my head, a tear spilled out of my left eye. Mr. and Mrs. Thompson had been like a second family to me. About six months after my mom died, Mrs. Thompson had caught me alone in the barn crying for no reason.

She never said a word, just put her arms around me and let me know she was there if I ever needed her.

Now she wasn't, I realized. There if I needed her. Both of them were gone and the tear was joined by many more.

Sara saw my head shake and knew the truth. We came together to cry in each other's arms. Giving solace and comfort while taking. As I held her, I thought of Luke all alone out there on the porch. He had no one to share this with. Even if he had. He wouldn't ever admit to feeling this pain.

Not Luke. The boy refused to show emotion.

My heart broke thinking about him having to go through this all alone.

Slowly the crying sobs slowed as Sara, and I held each other until she mercifully fell asleep. Sometime later, I also fell asleep, both of us on her bed.

That night I dreamed about Ryan running from a giant wave. The dream then shifted over to Haley stuck in a New York Skyscraper.

I woke the next morning to find Sara staring at me with red-rimmed eyes. "It wasn't a nightmare," she whispered. "Mom? Dad?"

I shook my head.

A lone tear spilled out as she took a deep breath and sat up in bed. "Luke?"

I almost smiled to myself. These two fought all the time. Sara hated how Luke was never ruffled by anything. She had to constantly fight to get anything. It all just came naturally to him. Loved at school. A dozen girls chasing him. Respected by the teachers. Smart, he never had to study but didn't really care about school. Star athlete who had planned on rodeoing this summer before going off to Oklahoma State on a football scholarship.

Wow, that wasn't going to happen, I realized. None of our planned futures were going to happen.

Typical brother and sister, I thought, pulling myself back to Luke and Sara. A constant spat. But no one, absolutely no one outside of the family, was allowed to hurt the other. For that, they would have to die.

I well knew the feeling. Ryan and I were like that. One of the many bonding moments between Sara and me. Older brothers. The bane of any girl.

"I need to check on him," she said as she got up out of bed.

"I sat with him last night," I assured her. "He will be alright."

Her brow creased. "I know he will be all right. It's Luke. But I still need to check on him."

50

Following her out to the porch we found him sitting on the wooden porch chair. He'd been in that chair for the last two nights. His pale wrist was laying across his stomach. He'd cut off the cast yesterday.

Had it really only been yesterday? The asteroid hit forty-eight hours ago. Two days. How had our world changed so much so fast?

I checked and saw that the sandwich I had made was gone, but something told me that Clancy had snatched it while Luke was sleeping.

"I'll take care of the animals," I told them then hurried to the barn. It hurt to be near them. I hated seeing Sara so torn up. It brought back too many memories. And I still had to worry about my family. Would I ever know what happened to them?

An empty coldness filled me. A bottomless hole ready to suck me in and never let me go. The depression was but a step away.

Filling buckets with the pump Luke had installed I refilled the trough. Let the chickens out and gave Clancy his two scoops of dog food. I was going to collect the eggs, but I realized that we should let them brood. A chicken in a few months was worth more than an egg today.

Unfortunately, I was done after only thirty minutes. Hesitating, I searched around for something to keep me busy. Anything instead of returning to the house and being swallowed by all that pain.

I curried Cimarron, Mrs. Thompson would have appreciated it. But I couldn't put it off forever and returned to the house. Both Sara and Luke were sitting on the porch staring at nothing. Both lost in their own world.

At least Sara had stopped crying. I knew she'd go back to it over and over for days. If not weeks.

That was how I spent the next two days. Quietly watching them. Taking care of the animals. Cooking for them. Well, not cooking. Things I could make without a stove. Sandwiches, salads, stuff like that.

I also conducted an inventory. No one asked. I just needed to know what we had and how long it would last.

The storm cellar was empty. There were four dozen empty mason jars on the shelf. But no food. This was modern times. People didn't need to stash food. It was stockpiled at the grocery store. You picked it up when you needed it.

My stomach clenched as I realized that was exactly what they were doing when they were killed.

But on the third day, Luke came into the kitchen, catching me making tuna sandwiches.

"The Mayo is going to go bad. We need to use it up."

Luke's brow furrowed as he stared at me, obviously trying to understand what I was talking about. As I watched the awareness begin to return, we were in a world of hurt and we needed to start making plans.

I had argued with myself if I should broach the whole survival topic with them.

Thankfully, Luke had come back. "I guess we need to start doing stuff."

I didn't scoff. I just nodded.

He let out a long sigh then turned and started emptying the freezer. "I'll set up the smoker. Make some beef jerky. Dad got it so we could smoke bacon when we harvested one of the wild hogs."

Biting my back teeth I nodded. We needed to do so much more but I didn't want to push him back into that darkness he'd just pulled himself out of.

"What else?"

"A garden? A big one."

He thought for a moment then nodded. "Shelter, water, food. I get it."

I could only nod. Then he suddenly got a pensive look, "Are you staying? I hope so."

My insides froze as I faced the choice I didn't want to face. "I think I have to. My dad said I should. I mean if it's okay with you guys."

"Yes, of course," he said as he started slicing the roast into thin strips. "I know if it had been the other way around, Sara visiting you guys. Your dad would have taken care of her."

Swallowing, I felt a relief fill me. I hadn't really doubted it. But in the back of my mind was an awareness that I was relying on the kindness of the Thompsons.

"Besides," he added with a small sad smile. "You know about this stuff."

"Dad and Ryan used to talk about it all the time," I said as I remembered the discussions around the dinner table. I had always rolled my eyes at them. But some stuff must have seeped into my brain. "They were always talking about the different ways the world could end and how the scenario might dictate what you did, when, and how."

He pushed his hat back on his head and looked at me for a long moment. Then nodded. "Okay, let me get the meat taken care of then the three of us will sit down tonight and figure out the next steps."

I pushed the fear back down below the surface where it could bubble and torment me. I hated not knowing the future. I hated not having a plan. Please, I silently begged. Please let us come up with a plan tonight.

Luke gave me a nod then turned to go start the smoker. I salted the meat and then wondered where we would get more salt. A body couldn't survive without salt. Especially not an Oklahoma summer. Suddenly I realized just how important the little things had become. They had been little and unimportant because they were always there. But take them away and suddenly they became super important.

I'd cook up the chicken breasts tonight. We'd use the last of the store-bought bread. Pulling out the flour, my world crashed again when I discovered only two cups worth remained.

A plan. We needed a plan for so many things. But one thing I now knew. This was my new home. I wouldn't be going to my Papa's in Idaho. The first step in a new plan.

Chapter Six

Luke

It took three loads to finish all the beef jerky. I wrapped up the cured meat in aluminum foil then plastic bags. But there wasn't that much, I realized. Two pounds, maybe. The rest had been water weight. It wouldn't last a week.

Cassie grilled the chicken and some corn on the cob then put a plate in front of Sara. "You have to eat," she whispered.

Sara looked up at her, then back down at nothing. Cassie frowned with a hint of fear behind her eyes. Her friend wasn't bouncing back.

My heart broke. Really, there was only one way out of this. Through. "Okay, that's enough," I growled at Sara.

She startled then looked at me.

"I know you're hurting," I said, toning down my anger. "We both are. I know."

She swallowed hard, not looking away. Something told me she was hoping for something, someone to push her out of the hell she'd fallen into.

Taking a deep breath I said, "I'm your brother. I need you, Sara. I can't do this all alone."

"Do what?" she snapped. "Nothing means anything anymore."

My brow furrowed as I stared at her. "How can you say that? Are you saying Mom and Dad lived for nothing? That all their sacrifices and hard work were for nothing. No. I refuse to believe it."

"Then what?" she snapped. "Why does it matter? We are all going to die anyway."

My heart ached seeing her pain. "It matters because we try to leave the world a better place. Think about it. Our lives are better than our grandparents. Or their grandparents.

"Not anymore," she scoffed. "We're right back to being where we were. Civilization is screwed. So what does it all mean?"

"Yes," I answered. "But now we know how to build stuff. We'll get back to where we were faster."

Sara rolled her eyes then stared down at her hands in her lap.

I ground my teeth in frustration. But Cassie saved me by taking Sara's hand and saying. "It means, your Mom and Dad were happier because you and Luke were in the world than they would have been if you had never been born. You made their lives better."

Sara looked at her friend and a small hope began to build inside of me when Sara didn't push back right away.

"But..."

"No," I said softly. "No buts. We are going to survive because if we don't then Mom and Dad really didn't matter. Out of all the people in the world, My parents will have their lines continue. I refuse to allow them to be pushed into oblivion. Forgotten by history."

Cassie frowned as she studied me for a long moment with a strange look.

"So," I continued. "It is imperative that my little sister lives. Not just tomorrow. Or for a week. But long-term. Do you understand?"

She studied her hands for a long second then nodded, just a little and I felt my heart beat again. My sister had taken the first step back to the real world.

"So, Miss Expert," I said to Cassie, "What are we missing? You've spent the last two days digging through every drawer and cupboard." I pointed to the black and white-speckled notebook.

She swallowed then said, "We need everything."

I did not roll my eyes, but it took effort. "Be more specific. I can't get everything."

58

She sighed again then said, "Food, a lot of food if we are going to survive, Food we can preserve and keep."

"Okay," I said as we nodded. "We are in farm country. It's got to be better than the cities."

She nodded but then looked pensively. "One of the things Dad always said was that when things went bad, people headed for the mountains."

"Like your brother Ryan," I said.

Her eyes widened, obviously surprised I had been paying attention.

"But this is Oklahoma. The nearest mountain is the Rockies three hundred miles to the west of us."

Cassie shook her head. "They are going to be searching for food."

My brow furrowed. "This is Oklahoma. It is almost all farms and ranches with the occasional oil well or Indian casino."

Sighing heavily, she said, "Think it through. There will be no more planting this year. Correct? Maybe never again. Not at the size and scale we used to have."

I nodded as my stomach began to clench up.

"The food from last year's harvest is in the siloes or already distributed to the processing plants, or in railroad cars."

Again I nodded, nothing she was saying was incorrect.

"So we are going to have to rely upon what we can get ourselves and keep others from taking what we have."

"Law of the jungle," I mumbled to myself, but Cassie heard me and grimaced. But she didn't correct me and say I was wrong.

"I can do the garden," Sara said. "I used to help mom. I know what to do."

My heart soared at seeing my sister contributing instead of wallowing in her pain.

"You should grow as much as you can," Cassie said, "What we can't eat we can trade. Beans, potatoes, starches, but anything else that you think will grow."

"I can get meat any time," I told them. "There are so many wild hogs down by the river. Mr. Jensen used to let Dad hunt down there to keep their numbers in check. Plus I can run a trot line for catfish."

Cassie nodded then explained about not collecting the eggs to let the hens brood out a new clutch of chicks.

"We should stop feeding them the chicken feed," I said. "There are enough scraps in the barn and fields for them. We need to make it last until harvest. Maybe into the winter."

"Winter?" Sara scoffed. "Do you think we will still be alive when winter comes? You're crazy."

I growled deep in my throat to stop from yelling at her. Instead, I leaned forward and said. "I don't know about you. But my parents didn't raise a quitter. If I'm not here come winter. It won't be because I didn't fight with every ounce of breath."

Sara balked and looked sheepishly at me from beneath her brow.

"I need you to be the sister I admired for her strength."

She blanched, obviously surprised I had thought of her that way.

"You have repeatedly overcome every obstacle put in your way. This is just another. I need you to face it and come to understand that you are strong enough to get past it. All of it."

A silent tear leaked from the corner of her eye. She quickly wiped it away then took a deep breath before nodding. "If Cassie has the animals, and me the garden. And if you expect us to survive next winter. Then you are going to have to plant corn."

Now it was my turn to look confused. "How? Nothing works."

"Like the Indians," Cassie interjected. "A stick makes a hole, drop in a kernel, move on. Between the manure pile and chicken coup we've got enough fertilizer."

My gut dropped as I realized I was going to end up becoming a farmer instead of a rancher. But I nodded. They were right. We would need corn, both for ourselves and for animal feed.

"Next thing," I said, "I'm going into town to pick stuff up before it all disappears. Give me a list of what you think we need."

Cassie frowned at me. "How are you going to pay for it? Money isn't going to be worth anything. And credit cards aren't going to work."

I froze as I was once again reminded of just how bad things had become. Then I smiled. "You said the towns are going to be short of food. Right?"

"Yes."

"Well then," I said with a smile. "A couple hundred pounds of wild pork should get us a ton of stuff."

Both girls hesitated, searching for a flaw or fault in my plan but failed to come up with a reason to stop it.

"We're coming with you," Sara said. Cassie nodded in agreement.

I started to tell them no but knew I would lose the argument so didn't even try.

The next morning I got two young boars. I saved a quarter for us, loading up the smoker with very lean bacon and hung a ham to dry. Then wrapped up the rest of the meat. The next morning the three of us headed to town with a hundred and twenty pounds of meat.

We were just down past our place when I made us turn off onto the Jenson's farm. Mrs. Jenson stepped out, shielding her eyes with her hand against the morning sun. An older woman in her late fifties. She was dressed in a cotton dress and apron. But the expression on her face made me hesitate.

Hope mixed with disappointment. I'd always liked her. She made the best oatmeal and raisin cookies and always insisted I take a bunch whenever I saw them.

Now she looked haggard and despondent.

"I was hoping you were my Paul," she said. Sara gasped next to me as we realized he hadn't come home.

"He was in Tulsa," she said, "John Deere was having a sale on combines. He was looking into upgrading."

My heart went out to her. Tulsa was thirty miles to the east of us. He should have been able to walk that far in the six days since the asteroid hit us. And I could see in her eyes that Mrs. Jenson knew it too.

"Here," I said as I opened my saddlebag and pulled out a ham and pork roast. "We can't eat all of this. Can you take it off our hands?"

She frowned for a moment then nodded. "I was worried. The freezer don't work. I haven't had any meat for a couple of days. You're Mom and Dad ...?"

Sara gasped then turned away to hide her tears.

Mrs. Jenson frowned. I grimaced then said, "Mom and Dad didn't make it. They were in the Win-Co when it got hit by that airplane."

Her eyes narrowed as she fought to understand. I think it was at that moment when she realized that her husband might not be coming home ever again. If it could happen to my Mom and Dad it could happen to him.

"If you need anything," I said to her. "Let us know. We're just up the road."

She stared off into nothing then nodded before turning and going back to her house. Confused, terrified, and lost.

I got the girls moving but I looked back and wondered how many people were like Mrs. Jenson. Alone in a new harsh world.

"What is going to happen to her," Cassie said. "They don't have animals. No crop in the ground. They don't even have a garden."

I shook my head, "Jenson was all farmer. A good one. But his interest favored machines. Anytime anyone around here had a problem with their car or truck. You talked to Mr. Jenson before taking it to a mechanic. Half the time he'd fix it then thank you for letting him work on your car."

We fell into a silence as I tried to figure out what was going to happen. But a new realization hit me as I felt a responsibility to Mrs. Jenson. She was a neighbor. But more. Who else out there needed our help? And what could I do without putting Sara or Cassie at risk?

"We'll stop and check on her on the way home. Maybe in a couple of days, one of you girls could take her a casserole or something. Find out how she is doing."

"Should we invite her to come stay with us?" Sara asked.

I shrugged, that was too far away and too big a decision. But something told me I'd be facing decisions like that in the future. The near future.

When we got to town I noticed how things had changed in only a few days. The wrecks had been moved off to the side. An old man and a little girl were driving an ancient buckboard wagon down the middle of the street.

People watched with obvious jealousy. The old man ignored their stares. But the little girl couldn't help but preen a little at being the center of attention.

There were two other horses tied up outside the Elk's lodge. Dad was a member and I was tempted to stop in and see what I could learn. How was the rest of the world doing? If anyone around here would know it was the Elk's, they had contacts everywhere.

But I pulled my focus back to getting what we needed and stopped in front of the drugstore. Old man Turner was outside with a sawed-off shotgun and a Colt .45 on his hip. Looking like a stagecoach guard expecting to be attacked by bandits.

He glanced up at the three of us and shook his head. "We ain't selling stuff. Only trading. Barter. The bank ain't taking deposits."

I nodded. "I've got over a hundred pounds of wild boar. Fresh killed yesterday. You interested?"

His eyes widened as he licked his lips. I could see him doing the calculations in his mind. He could use that meat himself or trade with others. Suddenly his eyes closed off as he shrugged. "Maybe," he replied. "What do you want to trade for?"

Before I could answer, Cassie jumped in, "Everything."

"I'm not giving you everything."

Again before I could say anything Cassie said, "Okay, let us load up a shopping cart. As much as we can get in it."

He frowned then shook his head.

Before she could answer him I swung Ajax around and said, "See I told you he wouldn't be interested. We'll have to take this stuff to Tulsa. They'll be hard up for meat already."

"No, No," he said then sighed heavily. "One cart for a hundred pounds of meat. It better be fresh."

I swung down from Ajax and tied him off to a truck mirror then grabbed the stuffed saddlebags. I nodded for Cassie to grab a cart then went into the store. He'd placed two storm lanterns at strategic spots.

After I dumped the meat on the checkout counter I grabbed a flashlight, filled it with batteries then used it to guide the girls.

They were in seventh heaven, gathering what they needed, dropping it into the cart. Picking up items then putting them back. Cassie made a beeline for the drug counter and loaded up on over-the-counter medicines. Vitamins, stomach stuff, tums, shampoo. Cough syrup and throat lozenges. Four bottles of aspirin and four of ibuprofen. She gave me a quick look and almost blushed then filled the bottom of the cart with girl things.

I turned away to pretend I didn't see and grabbed a bunch of toothpaste. We continued through the store. They had a small section of foodstuff. I smiled when I saw the round cans of cookies. They weren't that great. But I grabbed six of the cans for thirty pounds of shortbread cookies.

Sara stuffed two twenty-four packs of toilet paper on the bottom rail of the cart then we hit the candy aisle. "Hey, it's calories," Cassie said as she started loading up.

Sara hit the seed carousel and got everything she needed. Mom had a bunch at home. But having extra couldn't hurt. I noticed she went heavy on the beans. Plants that could give us calories.

We were almost full when I called Mr. Turner back to the pharmacy area. He shot me a frown.

"We need a bottle of Oxycontin and three bottles of anti-biotics. The kind that lasts."

His frown deepened. "You can't have those without a prescription."

I laughed then asked. "Do you think you will ever see prescriptions again? What you need a note from a doctor? Here," I grabbed a piece of paper from next to the cash register and wrote out, 'Give Luke Thompson a bottle of Oxycontin and three bottles of anti-biotics.' Then I scribbled an unreadable name at the bottom of the page.

"No meat unless we get these,"

He looked down at the paper then back at me. Both girls were staring at me, unable to believe I was being so demanding. But something told me that this stuff was going to be important.

"You know," I said, "In a couple of days when their supplies run out. The junkies are going to hit you up. And they're not going to take no for an answer. You might as well use that stuff to get what you need before you lose it all to people who are going to just come in and take it.

He continued to frown then finally he just shrugged and went back into the pharmacy. I was honestly surprised he hadn't been raided already. But we were out in the country. People hadn't gotten hard up yet. But it was going to happen. I just knew it.

"Grab some trash bags," I told the girls as I started to push the cart out of the store.

Mr. Turner stopped me and said, "Listen, if you need more stuff. I'll take all the meat you can get me."

I nodded, a good thing to know. But really, he didn't have anything more we needed. We'd gotten everything of value to fill our needs and I wasn't interested in opening my own store.

I filled my saddle bags, used two trash bags for everything else, and tied them onto Cochise.

Both girls smiled as we started back to home. I could see them both relaxing. We'd gathered what we needed. We were safe now. At least for a while.

Of course. That sort of changed when we hit the first roadblock on the way home.

Chapter Seven

<u>Cassie</u>

They'd put it up after we'd gone through. Four men behind wooden sawhorses at an intersection in the middle of nowhere. Farmland, telephone poles, and drainage ditches spread out from there.

Luke froze for a moment, his brow furrowing. "Hello Mr. Simms," he said.

The oldest of the men stepped forward, the three others, all in their twenties looked like his sons.

"Luke," the man said with a nod. "What you got there?"

Luke continued to frown. "Stuff."

I almost laughed at the curtness. Luke was not happy. I was about to say something when he shot me a frown, silently telling me to shut up.

"You aren't thinking about keeping us from going home," Luke said to Mr. Simms. "I mean, those barriers don't apply to us. Do they?"

I felt the tension rise as Mr. Simms's brow creased while he studied us. I noticed that he spent a long moment examining Sara and me. A moment long enough to send a slithering snake down my spine.

"No, you can go through," he said. "But we're keeping anyone else out. Someone took one of our steers yesterday. People we don't know keep passing through."

Luke leaned forward in his saddle then looked out over the flat farmland. "How you going to stop them?" he asked. "Someone can just go around you. Especially after it gets dark."

The older man's frown deepened. He obviously hated being corrected. Especially by a boy of eighteen.

Luke held his stare, raising an eyebrow, waiting for an answer. Finally, Mr. Simms shrugged and said, "If they try. We will shoot."

My heart jumped when I saw the seriousness in the man's eyes. He would kill someone without a second thought. What had our world become? Suddenly I realized there was no law. No one would report him booauoo thoro waa no longer anyone to report to.

Luke nodded then pulled Ajax to the side shoulder so he could go around the barriers. He didn't look back at us. He just expected us to fall into line. So of course, we did.

"We'll need you to help man the checkpoint," Mr. Simms said.

Luke looked back and said, "This isn't the right spot. The bridge over Bradford's

Creek would be better. Harder for people to get around."

The man's eyes grew three sizes as he clenched his jaw.

Luke spurred his horse up to a quick trot. Sara and I did the same to ours. I wanted to be away from there. The tension had been way too high for no reason.

"Why do you not like him," I asked as I drew up next to him.

He laughed then shook his head. "He looked down his nose at my dad. Dad had a day job, rented out his land. But he refused to rent to Mr. Simms, saying that Mr. Jensen treated the land better."

I nodded, a family feud. One more problem to deal with.

Sara leaned over to ask her brother, "His wife died last year. Right?"

He nodded with a tense jaw. We didn't stop at Mrs. Jensen's, instead rushing home. We spent the next hour putting everything away. I checked on the animals then came back.

Sara was preparing dinner and said, "We should have gotten flour, rice. He didn't have any but there should be some, somewhere."

Luke scoffed. "I'll get another hog in a couple of days and take it in. Start a list."

That became our life, me caring for the animals, Sara the garden, and Luke hunting and running the smoker.

He surprised me on the fifth morning by wrapping up some smoked bacon and saddling up Ajax to take the meat to Mrs. Jensen.

"Can I come," I asked. "I'm bored out of my mind and Cimarron needs a run."

He let out a long breath and I thought for sure he would say no, but he shrugged his shoulders, letting me tag along. Sara stayed behind. When we got there Mrs. Jensen stepped outside and I could tell instantly that Mr. Jensen still wasn't home. The woman looked harried as if she was holding on by a thread.

"Hi Mrs. Jensen," Luke said as he held up the wrapped bacon.

She smiled sadly when Luke handed her the package of meat then asked, "What are you going to do when you run out of pigs?"

Luke laughed then shrugged, "I was thinking about trying to put in some corn. I wish I had a mule, but I don't have a plow. Or seed corn for that matter."

Her eyes lit up as she beckoned for us to follow her. We both swung down from the horses and walked them behind her as she approached a large silver silo.

She started turning the wheel to raise the door at the bottom of the silo. "Preston sold off the last of our corn two months ago."

Luke nodded. Last year's crop had been forwarded to the mills long ago.

"But," she continued as she waved for us to look inside. "He hadn't cleaned it out yet. You're welcome to whatever you can get."

We both bent down to look into the door. Luke grunted his approval. There, spread across the concrete floor, was all the corn that hadn't been picked up by the auger.

"There is probably a hundred pounds," Luke said in amazement. "Don't you want to keep it?"

Mrs. Jensen shook her head. "You give me two hundred pounds come harvest and we're even. I figure I'm going to need it by then."

Luke smiled as he held out his hand to seal the deal then frowned. "Are you going to be okay? Here all alone."

The older woman took a deep breath then shrugged. "I am not leaving. Jeff Simms already tried to get me to come live with them. But no thanks. You get me that fresh corn in October."

We spent the rest of the morning filling three burlap bags with leftover corn. It was mixed with chaff and grit. Luke said we'd clean it when we got home.

The next morning I woke to find Luke already out in the fields with a hoe, digging a long shallow trench and dropping in seed, covering it, then moving on. At lunch, he was still out there. I had Sara make him some burritos and I took them out to him along with a jug of Kool-Aid.

He stopped when he saw me walking across the field, pushing at his back. "Thanks," he said as he took off his hat and wiped at his brow. He was covered in sweat and dust. And I will admit, looked very manly. Wide shoulders, working hard. I also noticed his rifle was leaning up against a fence post. He never went anywhere without it.

I bit down on commenting and refilled the cup with more strawberry Kool-Aid.

"How much are you going to do?"

He shrugged. "We've got enough corn for ten acres. But I think five will be enough. We'll save the rest for the chickens."

I could only nod. Five acres, with a hoe. It would take him a week or more of hard work. Suddenly I realized I wouldn't have done it. I'd have found an excuse. Or someone else to do it for me. I know, not one of my more prouder realizations about myself.

I became very aware of the tall boy standing next to me. Smelling like clean dirt and hard work. Suddenly, an awkwardness filled the air. It was so strange. Luke and I had never been awkward around each other. He hadn't ever been aware of my presence enough to make anything awkward.

But something had changed. Swallowing hard, I said, "I thought I'd take Cochise for a ride. He needs the exercise.

Luke nodded around a mouthful of burrito. "Fine, but stay on our property. Down to the river and stuff."

"Why? I thought I'd go up on the road, back away from town. We haven't been down that way."

I swear he wanted to roll his eyes but instead, he just sighed. "Please, just stay around the house where I can keep an eye on you."

My hackles rose, "Listen Luke ..."

He held up a hand to stop me. "I am too tired and sore to argue. If you go too far then I have to follow and keep an eye on you. And I've got too much work to do to be worrying about you."

An anger began to build inside of me, "I am not your responsibility. You don't have to worry about me."

He closed his eyes and slowly shook his head. "Yes, I do. That is my job, to worry about you and Sara. Please, just this once. Don't be a pest and do what I ask you."

I was about to protest when he used the ultimate comment.

"Just grow up a bit. You're not a little girl anymore. Pretend you're old enough to see I'm right."

My heart fell. Was he right? Was I being silly? A child? It had to be the meanest thing anyone had ever said to me.

My heart wanted to yell and stomp my feet but my brain was scrambling trying to find a problem with his statement. He was right. I was making a big thing out of something stupid. Cochise could get exercised just fine while staying on their property. A hundred and sixty acres was more than enough room.

I had just wanted to go for a long ride. Sara was pouting in her room. I just needed some freedom. But he was right. My stupid needs didn't trump his having to worry about us and I didn't need to make his job harder.

"Fine," I huffed then turned and stomped off. Just because he was right did not mean I needed to let him know I thought so.

When I'd gone about a hundred yards I turned to look over my shoulder and I could have sworn I saw Luke looking at my butt. He sort of blushed and quickly returned to hoeing the corn rows but I knew what I saw and I'll admit, a quick thrill shot through me.

I made a point of him seeing me exercise Cochise down by the river and back and forth over their fields. But I swear he made a point of his own by not looking at me and focused on his work. And no, that didn't piss me off to the ninth degree.

Let me tell you, being ignored can be particularly annoying.

Later that afternoon after I'd curried Cochise I was stepping out of the barn to find Luke, shirtless, bent over the water trough, dunking his head.

I will admit that I stood there, frozen for a long moment, unable to move as I admired the view.

He stood up and swept his wet hair out of his eyes then caught me staring at his broad chest.

The two of us locked eyes for the longest moment until I realized how silly I was looking and turned to hurry into the house.

That night I thought about the look in his eyes. It was a man's look. The way a man looks at a woman he finds pretty. This was stupid, I told myself as I turned over and punched my pillow. The world had just ended. My family was scrambling to stay alive. And I was getting all moony over a boy who didn't even know I was alive.

It was two weeks after the asteroid when everything changed again. Sara had finished planting the three gardens. Luke had finished with the corn. He'd only done three acres, I had two momma hens brooding two dozen eggs.

We were sitting on the porch. It got too hot in the house. Without air conditioning, it could become miserable, even with a cross breeze. The porch was covered by a thick oak tree and gave us nice shade in the afternoon from one or two o'clock on.

We'd just finished a meal of pork chili when Clancy stood up and faced the front gate. We all looked to see Mr. Simms getting down off his horse to open the gate then lead him up the long driveway.

I noticed that Luke moved his rifle to his other side then stood up. "Mr. Simms," Luke said as he nodded a welcome.

The man studied us for a long moment then shook his head. "I heard about your parents. I'm sorry."

Luke said, "Thank you," but I knew the man wasn't sorry and I knew Luke knew it also.

The man looked at me and Sara and I could see something behind his eyes that made me shiver. But he turned to Luke and said, "You lot need to move in with us. Can't have kids living on their own."

Luke frowned for a long moment then shook his head. "No, we'll be staying here."

Mr. Simms's jaw tightened. This was a man not used to being told no, I realized. "Listen, boy," he snapped. "You got two young women to think about."

Luke scoffed then said, "Thank you for the invitation. But we'll be staying here. We will be just fine. I've got three acres of corn in. Hogs down by the river. Chickens and Sara's put in a garden. We've got enough to live until harvest. We will be just fine.

Mr. Simms sighed heavily then shook his head. "We're getting more and more people at the barriers. It's going to get a lot worse. We need to stick together. From what I'm hearing, Tulsa has become a hell hole. People stealing. Food running short. They are going to swarm out of there, I'm telling you."

Luke nodded but he refused to back down.

I wondered for a brief moment if Luke was doing the right thing. Maybe we would be safer at their farm. What if we were swarmed by people from the city? But I could see it in Luke's eyes. This was his home. His parent's home. You couldn't get him out of there with a crowbar.

Then I saw the anger in Mr. Simms's eyes and knew Luke was doing the right thing. He hadn't asked us. But he was right.

Shaking his head, Mr. Simms turned to leave, but not before running his eyes up and down my body like he owned it. Luke noticed it as well and moved forward.

Mr. Simms looked up and realized he'd stepped over the line. I actually think he almost looked guilty but quickly shook it off and marched off the Thompson property.

When he was out of earshot, Sara shuddered and said, "If you go to the dictionary and look up creepy. That man's picture is right there."

We all laughed, but I couldn't stop thinking about Mr. Simms and what he said about the people in the cities. And what that might mean for our future.

Chapter Eight

Luke

The sun was coming up, painting the sky in red and yellows. Pressing my lower back, I twisted and stretched. My body still ached from putting in the corn. Reaffirming my decision to ranch instead of farm. But that plan had disappeared. Now it was just a matter of survival. Anything and everything revolved around that.

The screen door slammed behind me. I turned to see Cassie stepping out to join me. Suddenly my heart sort of skipped. I mean the girl was pretty. Cute type pretty. Her hair in a ponytail. Tight jeans. Yes, if we had been in school I might have chased her.

God, I realized. This was Sara's best friend. As out of bounds as a girl could get. Wrenching my wandering mind back to civilization, I gave her a quick smile, picked up my rifle, and headed to the barn. If I hurried I could be in place before the sun finished rising.

I was halfway across the yard when I looked over my shoulder to find Cassie watching me walk away. The strange look in her eyes confused me to no end. "Do. Not. Go. There." I mumbled to myself. Instead, I clenched my jaw and focused on my plans.

Slinging the rifle over my shoulder, I grabbed the wheelbarrow. I filled it from the barn manure pile then pushed it across the field to the far side of my corn patch. As I spread it I could only shake my head. This was going to take me forever.

There had to be a better way. I tried to think what Dad would do. But then I thought about my grandfather and smiled. The man had always been a tinkerer and there had to be a better way. I ended up cannibalizing mine and Sara's bikes. We hadn't used them in five years. I used rebar for the axil and built a six-by-four wagon out of spare lumber.

I hooked up a yoke. Filled the wagon and had Ajax pull it out to the field. It was the equivalent of ten wheelbarrows. He was not pleased. But I realized the horses were going to have to be trained in pulling things. Wagons, eventually a plow. There was just no way we could survive without their help.

It still took me three days to spread all our manure. I also made sure to take a load over to Sara's gardens.

After I was finished, I stood on the porch and looked out at my fields. Would it be enough? I wondered. I mean, how much food did we need? How much would it produce? I tried running the numbers and kept coming up confused. I just didn't know.

Maybe, we might make it. Especially with the meat I could add to the table.

The eggs, occasional chicken. Would it be enough?

That had become my worry as I realized mom and dad must have felt this all the time. If they didn't work, the kids starved. A new respect for them washed over me. It was a burden. This constant worry. Were we doing enough? What would happen if we failed?

There was no one to turn to. No government. No extended family. Neighbors in even worse shape. Sighing, I sat back on the porch and closed my eyes as I tried to figure out what else we could do. Water, Food, shelter, check, but what else? What was I missing?

Clancy rested his head on my leg, silently begging for his ears to be scratched. I laughed and accommodated him. The dog was good at reminding me to stop worrying. All I could do was all I could do.

As I sat there, I suddenly realized that the world had disappeared. I mean not only the former world and its civilization. But in this new world. We had no idea what was going on. Were they trying to fix things? Were we going to ever have electricity? The internet? Anything.

We were so cut off, the country could have been in the middle of a civil war and we wouldn't know. Hell, they could have nuked New York and we wouldn't have known. How much damage had happened after the hit?

We were so cut off. How were the towns and cities doing?

On the one-month anniversary of the asteroid hitting the earth, I noticed a dark cloud forming in the west and the wind shifting. We got most of our rain from the Gulf of Mexico, but this was coming in from the west.

A sick feeling hit me as I saw a distant spiral and yelled for Sara and Cassie. Both girls came out to join me on the porch as we watched the storm gather. Lightning flashed, dancing across the tops of black clouds bringing the distant rumble of thunder. The three of us stood next to each other, helpless.

"If it comes closer we're going into the storm shelter."

"The horses," Sara gasped,

"The chickens," Cassie added.

I didn't comment. Obviously, their lives were more important than the animals.

Thankfully, the storm shifted to the north but hit us with enough rain to turn everything into a muddy puddle. It'd take a day to drain off into the river. I silently cursed. There would be no hunting for a few days. The fields would become a quagmire of gluey mud.

Did my corn get set or had it all been washed away? My gut clenched, worrying I'd wasted all that work for nothing.

It took two days for me to get out into the field and find little green shoots popping up out of the dirt. A green carpet laid out over three acres.

Smiling like I'd just won the state championship at bull riding I almost danced all the way home.

Three days later I was down by the river searching for another hog when I spotted a group of people working their way along the bank of the river. My gut dropped as I realized these people had avoided Simms's barriers like I'd said would happen.

I stayed frozen next to a tree as I watched them. Seven. They looked like a family. Three adults, a couple, and an older man. Four kids ranging from seven to ten. Backpacks.

Smart, I thought, stay by the river. Suddenly a hog bolted from the underbrush. It's been spooked by the approaching people. They froze, surprised. I quietly swung to follow the beast. A good-sized hog.

Only when it was away from them and stopped to look over its shoulder did I fire. The hog dropped in its tracks.

I held my rifle on him, ready to shoot again if necessary. From the corner of my eye, I could see their shocked faces staring at me. Finally, I lowered my rifle then turned to them. "You're on private property," I said.

The woman gathered the children close to her. Both of the men stepped forward placing themselves between me and the rest of the family. All of them looked like they'd been put through the wringer. Nice clothes that showed too much dirt. The men needed a shave, the woman's hair looked like it had been styled at one time. Now it was too short for a ponytail and too long to ignore.

Sighing heavily, I started for the hog. The family watched me. Clancy walked next to me, keeping an eye on them.

Suddenly the man broke away from the family and started for mo. "Wo'ro juot passing through," he said as he looked at the pig then back up at me.

"Where you from?" I asked as I dropped down and started removing the insides.

"Tulsa," the man said as he watched me work.

I stopped and turned to him. "How bad is it."

His face turned a little white then he looked back at his family. "I got them out in time. Barely. Things were going bad. People were running out of food. The city, the cops, they're trying. But they don't have the food so people don't listen."

Again he looked down at the hog then back at me.

"We camped along the way," he added.

"Where you headed?" I asked. "Or are you lot just getting out."

He gulped then said, "My wife's family has a farm. In Lavern. Or just outside."

I nodded, a hundred and fifty miles. Glancing over at them I stopped myself from shaking my head. They probably wouldn't make it. If they didn't starve to death. The storms or some evil force would get them.

Hiking across Oklahoma without a gun. After what had happened. No, they weren't going to make it.

Suddenly one of the little girls started crying. My gut clenched up. God, the worst sound in the world is a child crying. Especially, that hungry cry. It will eat a man's soul.

"Tell you what," I said as I quickly quartered the two back legs with both hams. "You lot flushed him. Only fair you get half."

The man's eyes widened then narrowed as he searched for the trap. "You sure?"

"Take them," I said. "Only don't stop for another mile. There is a little bend in the river with some cottonwood trees and a nice beach. A good place to camp. No one can see a fire and there aren't any close farms."

He studied me, too afraid to make a move. But the woman wasn't, she hurried in and pulled one of the quarters back. The older man got the other.

"Thank you," she said as if she could not believe their good fortune. The sadness in her eyes was pushed aside by the sudden bounty. But I knew it would return again in a few days.

I nodded then said, "Make sure you cook them all the way. They might have trichinosis." I then swung the rest of the pig over my shoulder and headed for home. I was about fifty yards away when I glanced over my shoulder to find them gathering the heart and liver I'd left behind. Neither of the girls liked the innards.

Good, I thought to myself. Maybe they might make it after all.

When I got back I found Cassie up on the porch. She'd watched the whole thing. "Why do I think they won't be the last?"

I could only nod as I dropped my meat then started the smoker. A sick feeling started gnawing at my gut. Seven people had waltzed onto our property without me knowing. If I hadn't been out hunting they could have approached the house any time. If they had weapons they could have taken me out and I wouldn't have ever heard the shot.

Suddenly I realized just how vulnerable we were. Maybe Mr. Simms wasn't completely insane.

Chapter Nine

Cassie

I had just settled down. Sara was lightly snoring in her bed. I was still in a sleeping bag. Something we were going to have to fix. But no way was I moving into Mr. and Mrs. Thompson's room.

A sudden cackling of the chickens made me sit up. It was late. Almost midnight. My stomach clenched as I pulled on my jeans then my boots and raced out of the room.

I collided with Luke. It was like running into a granite cliff. He didn't budge. The both of us froze for a second. He was shirtless as he pushed past me. His rifle in his hand as he levered a round into the chamber.

"Stay here," he snarled as he pushed out into the yard. Clancy raced past us, barking like Satan himself had risen up from hell.

I, being me, ignored Luke. Something was after the chickens. A coyote? Fox? I didn't smell skunk. Badger? It could be anything.

The moon bathed the yard in silver light. Almost bright enough to read by. Suddenly, Luke slid to a stop and brought his rifle to his shoulder, and took aim. "Heel, Clancy," Luke yelled. "Now," he growled.

I peeked around him to see what was attacking my chickens. My heart fell when I saw a young boy racing out across the field holding one of my best hens by its feet. The bird clucking and flapping its wings. Cursing under my breath, I almost pleaded with Luke to shoot. My first instinct was to save my chicken. I am ever thankful I didn't say anything.

"Heel," he yelled again. Clancy looked at the escaping boy then back at Luke. Finally, he broke off his chase and returned to us. Luke raised his rifle and fired a shot up into the air. A way of letting them know we knew they were there.

The two of us stood next to each other watching someone disappear into the night with our property. Suddenly I realized I was standing next to a shirtless Luke who smelled of wood smoke and horse.

I then realized I hadn't had a bath in a month. I'd been using a washcloth to try and stay clean.

My stomach turned over. I was too afraid to move, or say anything. My mind was whirling, all I could think about was the boy standing next to me. Of course, he didn't know I was alive.

Cursing under his breath, he shook his head and said, "I was afraid of this." Just as Clancy came back, circled, he sat down next to his leg, his tail thumping the ground. Looking up at Luke for approval.

"What are we going to do?" I asked, glad that I could turn our conversation to something other than his broad chest or wide shoulders.

He turned then frowned as he realized I was there next to him. Snarling under his breath he shook his head. "Next time I say stay there. Stay there."

I sighed heavily. "We've already established you are not in charge of me. Something was after my chickens."

The look in his eyes sent a bolt of fear shooting through me. He wouldn't use physical force, would he? No, never. But a doubt wiggled around the bottom of my stomach.

His brow narrowed as he focused on me then said very carefully, "If you are unwilling to listen to me. Then I will have to ask you to leave our home. I can not have you getting in my way. You are going to end up getting somebody killed."

My stomach dropped. No, he couldn't be serious. Looking up into his eyes I realized he was very serious. My entire world shivered out of focus as I realized there was no one I could turn to.

Sara, I thought. No way would she allow this. Pushing past him I marched back into

96

the house to find her getting out of bed rubbing her eyes. She had lit a storm lantern, "What happened?"

Growling under my breath I told her about the boy stealing our chicken then I said, "Your stupid brother ..."

"What did he do this time?"

"He told me to stay behind," I growled through clenched teeth. "Then ... Then, when I followed him. He said if I didn't listen to him he was going to kick me out. Of your guy's home. Can you believe that? What right does he have? This is your house too.

Sara's forehead creased into a dozen lines as she slowly shook her head. "He's right."

"What?" I gasped. This could not be happening. "How can you say that? I thought you were my best friend."

"I am," she said and I could see the pain in her eyes "You will always be my best friend. You know that. But, don't ask me to take your side against my brother. Not when he is right."

My heart fell. She was supporting him. How could she do that? One more thing wrong with this new world.

"Cassie," she said with an exasperated tone. "Luke was having to make life and death decisions. Correct? I mean, from what you said, that boy could have been shot? Right? Or there could have been others."

"Yes, but ..."

"No buts," Sara said. "Were you ready to do that? I mean, if there had been other people. If they charged you and Luke. We're you ready to shoot them."

"I didn't have a gun."

She raised an eyebrow. "Who's decision was that? We've got two more rifles, a handgun and a shotgun."

I froze as I tried to think.

"No, you decided to rely on Luke to protect us. Right?"

Swallowing hard, I nodded, unwilling to say the words aloud.

"We'll, if we're going to put that responsibility on him. We need to give him the authority to do what he thinks is best."

My inside bristled at the thought of letting anyone be in charge of me. "But he threatened to kick me out. What would I do? Where would I go?

She looked at me for a long moment then said, "I'd make sure that didn't happen by doing what he says. Face it, he is in charge unless we want to take on the responsibility. And I don't want to have to kill people. Or worse, have to make decisions that might get someone I cared about killed."

I was going to continue to argue but something deep in my gut told me that at some point. Killing might be required.

A sadness washed over me as I realized that a wedge had come between me and Sara. I had always thought that impossible. Nothing could have ever come between us. Suddenly I realized that feeling was based on the old world. Where everything was easy, safe. We could afford to ignore the hard things and just focus on us.

Clenching my jaw, I turned away from her and crawled into my sleeping bag, turning my back to her, unwilling to face this hurt gnawing at my insides.

"Cassie," she said with an exasperated sigh. "I'm sorry."

I waved my hand over my shoulder then pulled a pillow to my chest and hugged it. I missed my family so much.

The next morning, Sara gave me a shy look, obviously terrified I was going to hate her forever. But I let out a long breath and gave her a quick smile, "We're good."

She relaxed and sighed heavily. "I just ..."

I held up my hand. "You were right, I was wrong. Now be quiet. Don't beat a dead horse."

She laughed then pulled me into a quick hug.

"Are you going to apologize to Luke?"

I pulled back, giving her my best frown. "No way."

She laughed and we were okay again.

When we got outside we saw Luke detaching the chicken coup from the barn. "What are you doing?" I demanded.

The chickens were scattered over the yard, clucking and demanding he leave their house alone.

"I'm moving this to the front yard. It's closer to the house."

On the other side of the house was a nice grass yard, forty by sixty surrounded by a white picket fence. The family spent all their time on the back porch or in the backyard. But Mrs. Thompson's mom had insisted on a nice yard out front, facing the road. With flower beds and green grass.

I don't think I had ever gone through the front door. If you had to get to the front yard for some reason you just went around the side from the back.

I can remember Luke grumbling about having to mow it saying they should just get a sheep or two to keep it in check. But Mrs. Thompson would just point and tell him to hurry up or she wasn't going to serve dinner.

"Why?" I asked him.

Grumbling under his breath he strained on a crowbar to pull the small coup away from the barn. Slowly it separated. It was only ten by ten. Just enough for a dozen birds, enough to keep the family in fresh eggs.

"There are nests in there,"

He ignored me as he lifted up the front end and started to drag it across the yard. Both Sara and I raced to help. That was how we moved the coup into the middle of their front yard. The birds would spend their time inside the fenced yard.

"And the horses are getting locked up in the barn each night." He looked down at Clancy. "And that's your new home. The barn."

The dog looked up at him and wagged his tail. Willing to help however he could.

I thought that would be it. But later that afternoon I found Luke stacking firewood against the side of the house on the back porch.

He caught me staring at him and shrugged. "Extra protection. That wood siding wouldn't stop a bullet."

My stomach dropped as I realized just how much danger we were in.

After he had every bit of wood and the lawnmower protecting the back he chained the gate at the road shut then all three of us pushed his old F-150 into place to block the driveway.

Unfortunately, when we were eating dinner that evening I saw him looking out across the fields and shake his head. "We're too open here," he mumbled more to himself.

"What do you mean?" Sara asked.

He froze for a moment and I knew he was debating with himself whether to say anything or not. Finally, he let out a long breath and said, "We are wide open to attack."

"Attack," Sara gasped. "Why would anyone want to attack us?"

He scoffed. "We have the most valuable things in the world."

"What?" I asked.

"Food, and two very pretty women."

My stomach fell as I followed his gaze out across the field. At the time I didn't even register that he had included me in the whole pretty aspect of things. Instead, all I could think about was how right he was. We were wide open.

Chapter Ten

Luke

My gut tightened as I stepped out onto the porch. A thousand evacuees from the city could have surrounded the house in the night. I wouldn't have had a clue. I couldn't stay awake 24x7 and no way was I asking the girls to patrol the grounds.

For the thousandth time, I cringed thinking just how open we were. There were no barriers to hide behind. Moving the chicken coup was too little. Maybe I could protect the birds. But not really. If someone wanted them, or the horses, or the girls. I would lose in the long run.

A determined group could take me out a dozen different ways. A long-range sniper. Burning the house in the night and shooting us as we rushed out. Or just plain overwhelming us.

The thought of joining up with the Simms sent a cold shiver down my spine. That might be worse. What about the rest of our neighbors? Should we all band together? Again I could only shake my head. Oklahoma farmers weren't known for depending on others. No, they'd all want to fight their own battles.

I continued to try and figure out some way to ensure we were safe and just couldn't. Not long-term. Not against everything.

Taking a deep breath, I shook my head then pulled up my chair to sip at my coffee and watch the sun come up. We were reusing the grounds to make them last. I hated to think what life would be like when we ran out.

Cassey joined me, pushing at her lower back. The girl really was coming into her own, I thought. She'd left that gawky coltish stage of all legs and taken on the curves of a woman.

"Morning," she grumbled as she massaged her back.

"You still sleeping on the floor? You can move into Mom and Dad's room tonight."

"What?" Sara gasped as she stepped out, letting the screen door slam behind her.

Cassie's face turned red as she shook her head.

I did not roll my eyes, but I wanted to. Instead, I said, "Sara..."

"What if they come back," she interrupted.

"Then we will adjust again. In the meantime..."

"No," Cassie said, "I couldn't sleep in their room."

"Fine," I said, "Then you can sleep in mine, I'll sleep in their room." Both girls stared at me, both searching for a problem with my solution and both coming up empty. I finished my coffee and took a deep breath.

"I'm going to get a hog and take some to Mrs. Jensen, Maybe the Sorrels will trade some corn meal for fresh meat. I don't want to go into town if I don't have to."

"Can we come," Cassie asked.

"I'll stay here," Sara said. "You can ride Brandy for me. She needs the exercise."

Cassie looked at me, raising an eyebrow.

I shrugged, "We'll go after lunch." Then I grabbed my rifle and headed down to the river hoping the hunt would be easier than the last few. I'd noticed the hogs were thinning out. I'd had to go an extra half mile to find them.

Either I was taking too many, or the slow trickle of people passing through was pushing them away. Unfortunately, they were gone. They'd disappeared like last week's wind. My stomach clenched. I'd counted on the wild hogs in my plans.

On the way back a cotton tail jumped out then sprinted down the trail. It made a fatal mistake and halted behind a bush. It was way overkill but a shot to the head didn't ruin the meat.

Later that afternoon with one cotton tail in my saddle bag, Cassie and I headed up the road. The sun baked us as a fine shimmer on the distant road reminded me that summer was coming on fast.

My stomach churned thinking about spending a summer on the Oklahoma plains without air conditioning. Glancing over at Cassie I noticed her quickly look away as her face turned pink. Why? I mean what was that all about?

When we turned off the road onto the Jensen's place my gut stiffened as a sense of wrongness hit me. Mrs. Jensen didn't come out to greet us. Cassie and I both sat our horses waiting.

Finally, I swung down and was approaching the door when it opened and a middle-aged man stopped out holding a shotgun. Mr. Jensen's shotgun I was pretty sure.

I froze, this was not Mr. Jensen. All of my senses went to full alert as I realized my rifle was still back in its scabbard on my saddle and my pistol was tied down on my hip. The guy had me if he wanted me.

"That's close enough," he said without pointing the 12 gauge at me.

"Where's Mrs. Jensen?" I demanded.

His brow knitted as he said, "That the old lady who lived here?"

"Yes," I snapped.

He pointed off to a small mound of earth next to the empty cornfield. "We found her. Dead. She left a note if you want to read it. Said she didn't want to stay around if her husband wasn't alive."

Cassie gasped from up on her horse.

My eyes narrowed as I studied the man. How could I know what he said was true? Who would investigate this? An emptiness filled me as I realized there was no one to figure out if sweet Mrs. Jensen had been murdered in her sleep or not.

"How do I know if you're telling me the truth?"

He shrugged. "You don't," he said as he patted his shotgun. "This says it don't matter."

As he continued to glare at me as the door behind him opened and a woman in jeans and a floral blouse stepped out, putting a hand on his shoulder. "We didn't kill her," the woman said.

An anger began to build inside of me. Frustration that I couldn't solve this problem. If they were murderers, there was nothing I could do about it. "So you just decided to take over her home?"

The woman shrugged, "We buried her. What's going on in Tulsa? She's lucky. They're just leaving bodies in the street."

I looked at the man, silently asking for an explanation.

He shrugged. "A gang war going on between two gangs and what's left of the cops. It ain't pretty. If you get caught in no man's land ain't no one coming to help you. We got out of there ten days ago. Ran out of food five days in. There's some here, but it won't be enough."

My heart raced as I tried to figure out what to do next. Cassie helped me calling my name, "Luke," she said then nodded that we should go.

Sighing, I looked over at the grave and shook my head. I was going to miss Mrs. Jensen. One more thing taken from my world. One more chunk carved out and tossed aside.

After I swung up on Ajax I leaned over and pulled out the rabbit and tossed it to the feet of the man, "Welcome to the neighborhood. Plant gardens. You might make it."

They both frowned, obviously neither had any experience. God, they were so clueless they didn't even know how much they didn't know. Not my problem, I told myself. I couldn't save everyone. Besides, We had our own problems.

I tipped my hat to the woman then pulled Ajax around and started back to the road. Cassie caught up and looked over at me.

"We've got enough meat."

She shook her head, "I wasn't questioning. I'm just surprised."

"Hey, I'm not a total jerk, despite what you might think."

Her face grew pink then she smiled. "Okay, but sometimes ..."

"Good," I said as I nodded, "Now that we know where I stand."

She smiled back and I thought she was going to say something else when distant gunshots echoed across the prairie.

"The roadblock," I cursed as I kicked Ajax to get him going. Cassie rushed after me, and the both of us leaned over our horse's neck as we raced down the road's shoulder. I pulled back on Ajax and shucked my rifle from its scabbard as we drew closer.

A sick feeling of unknown worry filled me as I saw two bodies, on the other side of the barrier. On this side, Mr. Simms lying on his back, a pool of blood spreading out from beneath him, his soulless eyes staring up at the sun.

On the side of the road, his youngest son, Garret sat with his head in his hands shaking like a leaf on a tree. His pistol on the ground next to him.

"What happened," I asked as I continued to scan the area for any more threats.

Cassie's mouth dropped open as she stared at the bodies lying in the road.

"Here," I snapped as I swung down and handed her the reins. "Garret," I said as squatted down next to him. He'd been two years in front of me in school. Never a jerk, just another upperclassman. Played basketball, had a girlfriend named Jenny, I think.

"Garret," I said again as I gently touched his shoulder. "What happened."

He looked up with red eyes, lost in his own personal hell. "Dad ..." He began then gulped trying to regain control. "They came up, refusing to stop, they just kept coming."

I nodded, encouraging him to continue.

"Dad ... Dad threatened them. He told them. I heard him. But they kept coming. One started to raise his gun. Dad ... Dad shot him. It ... it happened so fast. Dad shot. He... I don't think he meant to fire. The gun went off. The man fell. His friend shot Dad. I shot the man who shot Dad."

My stomach clenched up. Three dead men. Why? Why hadn't they just stopped and turned around? Why couldn't Mr. Simms just let them through? Why did they have to die? Why did Mrs. Jensen die? A mule kicked my gut as I thought about Mom and Dad dying. How many would die before it stopped?

"What do I do?" he asked.

A weight settled on my shoulders. How was I supposed to know? I was eighteen. Why did I have to solve his problems? But an image of Dad frowning at me made me take charge. "We'll take your dad back to your place." I swung to address Cassie. "We'll use Brandy. You can ride double with me."

So that was what we did, Garret and I got his dad up over Brandy's back. She wasn't happy about it. No horse I ever knew enjoyed the smell of blood. She sidestepped us trying to get away but Cassie held her in place and we got the body up and over then tied him to the saddle.

I looked at the two men in the road and shuddered, Mr. Simms first, I thought as I handed the reins to Garrit to lead the horse then got up on Ajax and held out a hand for Cassie, She used the stirrup and swung up behind me.

When her arms wrapped around my stomach I sighed and just let myself enjoy it for a second. The smell of her rose scented shampoo hit me.

We slowly walked the two miles back to the Simms's place. The three other brothers rushed out. Their faces drained of color as they realized what had happened. Marvin glared at his younger brother. "Who did this," he yelled then turned to his brothers, "Get your guns."

"There's no need," I told them. "They're dead. Garrett made sure of that."

The oldest brother looked at his younger brother and let out a long breath. While they were dealing with the body I examined their place and shook my head. Just like us, they were wide open. Obviously, that was why Mr. Simms had chosen to set up the roadblock, hoping to keep people away from his place.

How did that work out for him? I wondered.

"Thank you," Marvin said as he handed back the reins.

Cassie gasped from behind me and said, "I can't ride her." The saddle was covered in blood.

"We'll clean it when we get home," I told her and turned my horse. Making sure to cut across the Simms property. If I didn't return

113

to the roadblock I wouldn't have to deal with those bodies.

I know. I know. Not very noble of me. But I wanted to get home. Sara was there all by herself and too many people were dying around there. Besides, I didn't want to spend the day digging two more graves.

Cassie hugged me tighter as I worked us up to a trot. Ajax shifted lead and Cassie gasped as she began to slip. I reached back behind me, my hand grabbing her hip to keep her in position.

I nice firm, curved perfectly, type hip.

When I realized she was not going to fall off I let go and returned to getting us home. But not before I felt her rest her head against my back. Okay, A guy could get used to this.

Sara was on the porch, her hand shading her eyes as she watched us come down the path. She gasped when she saw all the blood on the saddle. Then her eyes locked on Cassie's arms wrapped around my middle and I swear her eyebrows rose three inches.

Cassie hopped down then quickly explained what had happened. I will not admit I felt a bit of a loss. But I won't deny it either.

That evening as we sat on the porch a new awareness began to sink in. We were vulnerable. Suddenly a thought began to creep into the back of my brain. Without thinking, I got up and found the book from Dad's shelf and brought it back out onto the porch.

I shifted the storm lantern and began to read.

"What are you reading?" Cassie asked.

Taking a deep breath I held it for a moment, debating with myself to say anything or hide my thoughts. Finally, I looked up from the book and said, "It's one of Dad's books. He had a passion about Western history."

Both Cassie and Sara laughed. It had been a known thing. If you needed to get Dad a present, get him a box about the old west.

"So, what is that one about."

"The Chilsom trail," I said then held my breath expecting a gasp at the implication. But instead, both girls frowned as they studied me.

"Why," Cassie finally asked.

"The trail," I said, "It wasn't really a trail. Just weigh points, watering stops for cattle drives. From Texas up to the rail yards, or up to Montana."

"Again, Why?" Cassie asked and I could see the worry behind her eyes.

"Because," I said, "Just in case."

Cassie sighed in frustration. "Again, Why?"

My stomach turned over. Saying it aloud might make it come true and I so didn't want to have to do this. But denying it wouldn't make it go away. "Because, if we have to abandon this place. I figure the next best place would be a farm up in the mountains of Idaho."

Chapter Eleven

<u>Cassie</u>

The memory of those men lying on the road would not leave my mind. Sighing, I turned over and stared into the dark. I was lying in Luke's bed. Words I never thought I would say. It smelled like him. Sara had washed the sheets while we were gone and they still smelled of a dry wind. But the room smelled of Luke. Not bad. Leather, smoke, and his dad's Old Spice.

I will admit. A bed was so much nicer than a month on a sleeping bag. I wondered how he was doing in his parent's room. Sleeping peacefully, I prayed. He deserved it. He worked so hard.

And I knew he was feeling the weight of being in charge. Always on alert. Always worrying about having to make the right decision.

I cringed inside thinking about how I challenged him when he told me what to do. I ended up just making his life harder. Today had been a lesson of how bad things could go. And how fast. Three men dead.

An image of Luke was replaced with an image of Mr. Simms lying over Brandy's saddle. There was so much blood. I didn't know there would be so much blood. A cold fear flowed through me as I realized death was forever. Mr. Simms would never see his grandchildren. Never laugh, nor smile.

He was lying buried in the ground.

God, a fear filled me. I did not want to die.

Biting my lip, I forced my mind to pretend I hadn't seen those men. Focus on something else. Please, something else.

Wrapping my arms around Luke while we raced across the fields popped into my mind and made me smile. Yes, a much better thought. He felt so solid. So male. And then, when I'd almost been tossed off he'd reached around and grabbed my butt to keep me there.

Okay. A special memory.

That was followed by the memory of Luke reading the book. Was he serious? No, it was impossible. Going to Idaho. Dad said to stay here. We were safer here. Right?

My mind worried the problem into the night. I woke the next morning from a sweet dream of a faceless boy petting a faceless dog. When I came out I found Sara and Luke arguing about who should get the water for the toilets.

"I'll get it," I said as I pushed passed them.

"No," Sara snapped. "It's his turn."

He rolled his eyes and said, "Fine. Jesus, you'd think I'd killed her dreams. She's been snapping at me ever since we got home."

I looked at Sara and saw her blush. A for sure sign he'd hit the mark and she was feeling guilty. Why was she mad at him? The water was just a symptom. I was still trying to figure it out when she shot me a frown and I realized she was mad at me also.

After Luke left to get the water I asked her, "Why are you upset at me?"

"I'm not," she said, obviously lying through her teeth. Sara was a terrible liar.

"Sara?"

Sighing heavily, she said, "You and Luke. My best friend shouldn't be hugging my brother."

"Sara," I gasped, suddenly terrified Luke would step back in and hear her stupid silliness. "I was riding behind him. I couldn't sit in Brandy's saddle. It took me two hours to clean it."

Her brow furrowed. "Was that all it was? It didn't look like that."

"Come on Sara. Luke barely knows I'm alive."

She continued to frown. "So you're telling me you're not interested in him. No crush, or anything like that."

"No," I told her. "Never." Of course, unlike Sara, I am a very good liar.

She continued to frown at me but we were interrupted by Luke coming back in with a five-gallon bucket full of well water. He frowned at us, obviously trying to figure out what we were talking about.

I pushed past him so I could check on my chickens and prayed Sara dropped the whole thing. No way did I want her finding out I had a crush on her brother. In fact, if I was honest. I'd had a crush for the last four years or so. Sara and I had watched him in Junior Rodeo get bucked off a bronc. He'd jumped up, embarrassed. But, I'd fallen like a ton of bricks.

Later that afternoon I found Luke in the shade of the big oak tree again reading his book about the trail going north. He caught me frowning at him and shrugged.

"Just in case."

"Do you think we might have to?"

Again he shrugged. "I don't know. Maybe. It depends."

"On what?"

"On how desperate people get."

"But won't we be in danger? On the trail. I mean it's what? Fifteen hundred miles? On horseback?"

Taking a deep breath he nodded. "Yeah. But we might not have a choice."

A heavy silence fell around us as I tried to understand. "But what about before? I mean in the old times. How did people survive out here? I mean there were Indians, outlaws."

"A lot of them didn't survive. There also weren't the numbers of people. And they hadn't been thrown into chaos with no backup plans. No way out. My gut tells me that they are going to come out of places like Tulsa searching for food."

His brow knit with worry then he added. "I had a dream last night. People overwhelming us like locusts. Just crowds and crowds of them. I couldn't stop them. Sara, ... Sara and you were trampled under the crowd. The crowd always moving, like a river of people."

My insides froze with fear as I saw his vision. No, it was impossible.

"Should we get ready? I mean pack?"

He thought for a moment as he stared off into the distance then nodded. "It wouldn't hurt."

We sat there in silence as the new reality began to sink in.

"Just because we get ready doesn't mean we have to go. But if we do, we won't have time to prepare."

I swallowed hard then nodded as a thousand thoughts danced through my mind. What if Dad came here looking for me? But, I would get to see Ryan, my cousins. Would they have gotten to my grandfather's?

I pushed up and started for the house.

"Where are you going?" Luke asked.

"To pack," I told him.

He nodded then sighed heavily. We both felt it. This movement. This inevitability. This unknown future that held so many unanswered questions.

That was how I spent the next two days. Packing. We discussed it and determined that Sara and I could take fifty pounds of supplies each. Cochise could pack 200 pounds. So it became a game of Tetris, putting different combinations together. Comparing the value of food next to gear. A ten-pound tent meant less food. We would also have to pack oats for the horses and dog food for Clancy.

Sara had loaded the dining room table with all the food to divide up. But I found her staring out the window.

"What is going on?" I asked

She sniffed then nodded to her gardens. "It isn't fair. I worked so hard. The beans are just coming up."

I squeezed her shoulder and thought about the cornfield Luke had put in. Two weeks of back-breaking work all for nothing.

"We don't know that we are leaving," I told her.

She shot me a look like I was insane. "Luke wouldn't be going through all this if he didn't think it was going to be necessary. And you agree with him."

"You don't?" I asked, surprised.

"I don't know," she shrugged. "But I do know that you agree with him. Things have changed. You used to disagree with everything he said. Now you are always on his side."

"Oh, Sara. I don't know if going to Idaho is the right move. But it can't hurt getting ready just in case."

She studied me for a long moment then returned to sorting food. We ended up separating out the last two pounds of corn meal. The five-pound bag of flour. The cooking oil. All the smoked meat and beef jerky. Maybe six pounds. Three cans of peaches. All the sugar and coffee we had left. And four pounds of dried pasta noodles.

"It isn't much," I said. "not enough to get us to Idaho."

Sara nodded. "If we stayed we could add to it from the hogs and fishing in the river. We'd have enough to last until harvest."

I swallowed hard as I realized that if we stayed, we'd have enough to survive. At least until someone tried to take it away from us.

Shaking my head, I started gathering the gear. A cast iron skillet. Three sleeping bags. A tarp. The smaller four-man tent. Two changes of clothes each. I started going through all the supplies we'd gotten from the store in town and shook my head. We would have to leave so much behind.

I packed at least one of everything. I put together a first aid kit. Including the painkillers and antibiotics Luke had gotten and prayed, we never had to use them.

While we were working, Luke made a pack for Cochise out of 1x6s that he could use to hang our gear. He also put aside forty pounds of oats and ten pounds of dog food.

We were putting it all together in the living room. Luke wanted it all in one spot so we could get it fast if we needed to. The three of us stood there looking at it, each lost in our own thoughts about how little it was to go so far.

"This is stupid," Sara said as she shook her head.

Luke let out a long breath then said, "Maybe."

My insides cinched up. If we had to do this. Then things had gone real bad. Were we jumping from the hot pan to the fire? No, if we left, it would be because we had no other choice. It was leave or die.

I was about to tell them we should have fried chicken for dinner. If we were leaving we couldn't take the birds with us. But I was interrupted by Clancy barking like the devil himself was rising from the earth.

Luke grabbed his rifle from beside the back door and raced outside. Sara and I followed.

He motioned for us to stay back then hurried to the truck parked across the driveway. A dozen people were up on the road. My heart hurt. They looked so bedraggled. Like they'd come out of a washing machine's spin cycle. Two women. Ten men. Most dressed in Jeans. One of the women didn't have a hat and her skin was bright red from the sun.

There was only one backpack between them. Another man had a small suitcase he was dragging on its wheels.

My heart raced. Twelve people. Why so many? Where did they come from? The barricade, I realized. It wasn't manned anymore. The Simms must have abandoned it. People were getting through.

I noticed two of the men had rifles. They stared at Luke who stared back.

A middle-aged man in his forties stepped up and rested his hand on the chained gate. "You got any food. We'll work for food."

Luke let out a long breath, then shook his head.

I could feel the tension rising as one of the women pointed to our chickens. Several of the men were looking around like they were searching for unseen threats. Either that or for some way to attack us.

My insides were all jumbled up. Luke was out there all alone facing off against ten men. At least two of them were armed. I thought about the dead men at the barricade and worried that Luke was going to make the wrong move.

Suddenly the screen door slammed as Sara stepped out. I hadn't even heard her leave. She handed me the shotgun then levered a round into the rifle and stomped off the porch to join her brother.

Aghast, I hesitated then rushed to join her, slightly embarrassed that I had been slow. We stepped up next to Luke behind the hood of the truck. Making sure the people on the road saw our weapons.

Clancy stood off to the side. He'd stopped barking and was waiting for a command.

My insides tumbled over themselves as I tried to stop my hands from shaking. I made sure not to put my finger on the trigger, suddenly terrified I would shoot someone unintentionally.

Or worse, get Luke or Sara killed.

"We don't have any food to spare," Luke told them. "Sorry. But you might try down by the river. Two miles further, the Anderson Bridge crosses over. On the other side is a nice fishing spot."

"We don't have gear."

I knew instinctively that Luke wanted to roll his eyes. How could people leave their homes in the countryside and not bring fishing gear? I wanted to mention to him that we hadn't included any in our gear either. Something I would remedy later.

"Cassie," he said. "Go get my rod and some hooks. In my closet."

The man's eyes opened as he took a step back from the fence. I left the shotgun leaning up against the truck and raced back to the house.

I rushed in and found Luke's rod and spinning reel. His tackle box gave me a packet of small hooks. I was hurrying back when I slammed to a halt and saw the two dozen eggs on the counter. Snatching them up I hurried out, making sure not to spill the eggs.

Luke's brow shot up when he saw me with the eggs but he sighed then nodded for me to take them up to the fence.

I approached and felt my heart drop as I got closer. They looked so not right. Scratches and soars. Ripped clothes. These people had been living rough for weeks. But it was the smell that hit me. They hadn't washed in forever. That sour body smell of too many days without soap.

Holding my breath, I handed the rod to the man and the eggs to the red-faced woman. Then for some unknown reason, I took off my cowboy hat and put it on her head. The sad look of relief will haunt me to my dying day. Nobody should look that grateful for a stupid hat.

Her eyes told the story. Fear mixed with misery. A simple gesture of kindness had rocked her world. As if she never expected to see kindness again.

Stepping back, I put my hands in my back pockets. Suddenly unable to fathom this new world. People begging for food.

Middle-class people. Accountants, teachers, IT experts. Regular people, reduced to this.

A realization of what my life would have been like if I hadn't been at the Thompsons when the asteroid hit. There but for the grace of god go I.

Swallowing hard, I went back to stand next to Luke behind the truck but I didn't pick up the shotgun. Instead, we stood there watching them walk down the road.

What was their story I wondered. Had they started out together? Or had they come together on the road? What would happen to them? Would they survive? Or die of starvation along the way?

A new reality hit me. What would I do if I was starving? Would I steal? Would I kill to get food? What if it was Luke or Sara dying? What would I do to save them?

Luke turned to me and I saw it in his eyes. The same thoughts. What were we willing to do to stay alive?

Chapter Twelve

Luke

I thought I was ready. I really did. I had done the work mentally, preparing myself. My gut told me we were going to get hit. There were too many desperate people and they all seemed to be coming for us.

For two days I got ready. Prepared to fight. This was our home. No way was I letting anyone take it from us. But at the same time. There were Cassie and Sara to think about. If this had been the old west I would have moved them to the nearest army fort then come back.

It was early evening. Just past sundown. Still, enough light to see stuff but the air had lost its heat. A soft breeze out of the north and the crickets were going full blast.

Clancy set it off. Barking and growling in the barn. I grabbed my rifle and raced across the yard. Bursting through the door I found a big man pulling at Cimarron's halter while Clancy tore into his other arm, trying to pull him away from the horse.

I stood there in shock until he dropped his hold on the halter and pulled a pistol from a hip holster and pointed at Clancy. The dog was shaking back and forth tearing into the man's arm. He was having trouble getting an aim at my dog.

Then he looked up and saw me. His aim shifted from my dog to me.

I didn't hesitate and shot him. The bullet hitting him in the chest. His eyes widened in shock as he looked down at the blood spurting out then up at me, unable to believe what had happened. I watched as the realization hit him. He cried out for someone then slumped to the ground.

Clancy backed off looking at me then at the dead body on the ground.

My body shivered as I fought the adrenaline rushing through my body. I had to, I kept telling myself. He was going to kill Clancy and steal our horses.

I was staring at him, unable to believe what had happened when a scream from the house brought me back to reality. I raced outside to see Cassie being drug across our yard towards the river.

Two other men were coming out of the house, their arms loaded with our food. One had a shotgun. A ten gauge like Mr. Jensen's.

Without hesitating I brought my rifle to my shoulder and fired at the man dragging Cassie. His head exploded. A 30-06 will do that to a skull at twenty yards.

The two men on our porch stared at their friend then back at me. I jacked another round into the chamber and was preparing to fire when our shotgun exploded from inside the house. The man with Mr. Jensen's gun was lifted up and thrown off the porch like a leaf in the wind.

Man number four dropped his haul and raced towards the road. I fired and missed then fired again and missed again. Before I could reload he was over the fence and into the far ditch.

I stood there, unable to move. Unable to believe what had happened. Two minutes earlier I had been regular Luke. Now I was a killer of men. My stomach clenched as this new reality hit me.

Then I saw Cassie getting up off the ground wiping the blood from her face. She stared down at the man who had dragged her out of the house then kicked the body in the ribs. Her hands curled in fists as if she wanted to punch him again.

I turned to see Sara step out the back door, smoke drifting up from the barrel of the shotgun. She looked at the body in the yard. The man she'd killed then at me. Her eyes had a lost look.

A part of her had died, I realized as my heart broke. We shouldn't have to go through this. It wasn't right.

I gathered up Cassie and put my arm around her shoulder and led her to Sara where I could hug them both.

Sara started crying, that ugly cry where she couldn't catch her breath. "I ... I had to wait ... the shotgun. In the other ... other room."

"Shush," I told her as I rubbed her back. "You did the right thing. Perfect. You saved us."

Cassie buried her head in my chest and whispered, "Thank you. He had me. I ... I couldn't get away."

"You're safe now," I told her as I squeezed her, letting her know she was okay.

We stood there like that for ten minutes, unable to believe how our lives had changed once again. We had killed to protect our own. We weren't the same people.

Taking a deep breath, I looked off into the distance and felt my gut tighten. Light on the horizon. A fire. Where the Jensen's place would be. Swallowing hard, I looked at the man's shotgun on the ground and knew what had happened.

Then a long column of smoke rose from the Simms's place. A flicker of light told me that place was burning also.

"We should go," Sara said with a sniffle. "We can't stay here."

"Sara?" I said as my mind fought to deal with it all. Leaving was quitting. It would mean abandoning our family's heritage. But those fires told me the truth. We were going to be overrun.

"No," Sara demanded. "We can't stay here. They will get us next time. And we know there will be a next time. There are too many of them. I've been counting. Forty-nine on the road and two dozen down by the river."

I hesitated. She hadn't seen the fires but she already wanted to go. This was such a big step. Would we be safer going to Idaho? What if we got there and things weren't better? We'd abandon what we had for something worse.

"That's in two days," Sara continued. "What happens next month when things get worse? And the month after that. Thousands and thousands of people will be swarming the countryside looking for food. How many will we have to kill?"

Taking a deep breath, I pointed to the distant fires. Both girls blanched as they realized. Pulling back, I looked at Cassie, raising an eyebrow, asking what she thought.

Her brow furrowed as she looked up the road then to the north. I could see her thoughts. Her family was up there. But there would be so much danger along the way.

But would it be worse than here? How could it be? I'd been lucky. We'd killed three men. Next time we wouldn't be that lucky. What then?

What would I do, I wondered. If I was them. The people coming out of the towns and cities. If my family was starving. Chickens, crops. Hell, I'd eat a horse if I had to. If it meant keeping my family alive one more day.

"We're going," I told them and felt a sense of relief. I'd made a decision. "Now, before they get here." We now had a goal. A quest. An adventure to meet. Was it the right thing? I would never know.

Both of the girls stared up at me, silently questioning. I could see it in their eyes. Was this smart? But both of them nodded, accepting my decision. I really think the three dead bodies made it easier for them. The new reality could not be denied.

"Tonight?" Cassie asked.

"Yes," I told her then saw the blood still on her face. "Wash up. I'll get the horses ready."

Both girls balked and now that the decision had been made they were having second thoughts. "Hurry," I told them. I didn't know if the men who had attacked us were the same ones who had set those fires, taken the shotgun from the people at the Jensen place. I didn't know anything. I just knew we had to move.

I'd just finished saddling Brandy for Sara when the girls stepped out. Cassie hesitated for a moment then rushed around to the chicken coup and spilled all of their corn onto the ground.

She caught me watching her and shrugged then helped me load Cochise's pack. When we were done I held their horses as they mounted then swung up on Ajax. I hesitated as I looked at our farm.

It had been in my family for a hundred and thirty years. Before the Sooners. Bought from the Osage tribe by a distant ancestor. And I was abandoning it. My gut tightened in shame and guilt.

Distant gunshots pulled me back to reality. The Sorrel place south of us.

"Let's go," I said as I nudged my horse towards the river. An anger built inside of me when we rode through my cornfield. So much hard work was being abandoned. So much future food.

Cassie trotted up next to me and reached out to touch my arm. "We're doing the right thing."

I scoffed then looked over my shoulder. We were running away.

But, I reminded myself as I looked at the now three fires on the horizon. We were getting away.

We were half away across the field when gunshots rang out. Close shots. From our home type close.

I instinctively ducked then looked back to see three men in our yard firing at us. Something told me one of the men was the guy who had gotten away. Spurring Ajax I rushed towards the trees lining the river.

Both girls leaned over their horse's neck, showing as little profile as possible as shots continued to ring out.

It was only when we reached the trees that I was able to relax. I held my breath as I examined the girls, terrified I would find them full of bullet holes.

But they looked back, as shocked as I was to find that we hadn't been hit.

Every instinct told me to go back and kill those men. They had threatened me and mine. But Cassie saw me pull Ajax around to go back and put a hand on the reins as she shook her head.

"We need to go."

I ground my teeth then finally nodded. So I turned us west.

"Why not the roads?" Sara asked.

"Fewer people," I told her. "And if we try to go across country we'll run into constant fences. Here we can move safely."

She nodded then sighed and looked over her shoulder. I knew she was thinking about the man she had killed. We had rushed so fast she hadn't had time to process it all. It was obviously starting to settle in.

"Thank you," I told her.

Her brow furrowed. "For what."

I laughed like she was being silly. "For saving my life. That guy was going to kill me. I was turned the wrong way. He had me. If you hadn't shot him I'd be dead."

A relief seemed to settle over her. And yes, I'd stretched the truth. But my sister didn't need to beat herself up over killing that man.

We continued on as day fell away into darkness. A large silver moon gave us enough light to make our way. It was midnight before I found a sand bar next to the river.

"We'll camp here," I told them. Both girls looked back at me, too tired to complain. We set up a quick camp. No fire, just a tent. The horses were staked on grass.

The four of us climbed into the tent and were out within minutes.

I was relying on the horses or Clancy to warn us if anything approached.

The day finally hit me like I'd run into a brick wall. Killing those men. Being shot at. Abandoning everything I knew. All of it washed over me, pressing me down, making me feel small and useless.

I was fighting against the doubt and pain when I thought about our goal. The mountains of Idaho. A place we could protect. Somewhere we could survive. A sanctuary. That was our goal. Our quest. Get there and live.

Chapter Thirteen

Cassie

I woke curled up next to a furnace. Luke was behind me, his knees tucked in next to mine. His hard chest put out enough heat to warm the entire tent. All three of us were in our sleeping bags, but I could still feel him behind me.

Sighing, I let myself enjoy it. This sense of rightness. But Clancy lifted his head and glanced at me, slamming his tail into the ground twice.

Nature called, So I carefully slipped out of my bag and out of the tent. Clancy joined me as I rushed to the bushes. The sun had come up an hour earlier. The high blue sky let me know it was going to be a scorcher.

Taking a deep breath, I sat on a log and stared into the distance. Clancy sat down next to me, demanding I pet him. Absently scratching behind his ears I thought about the last twenty-four hours. I hadn't dealt with what happened. Too much, too quickly.

My stomach clenched as I remembered the fear that tore through my body as I was being drug across the yard. I'd twisted and pulled, screamed and yelled. But the man was too strong. Too big. He'd ignored me like I was nothing more than a kitten on a leash.

A small nothing that he controlled completely.

A thousand fears had washed through me then his head exploded. I will never forget the feeling of hot blood hitting my face. Not warm. Hot. Then the body collapsing and seeing Luke there, the rifle to his shoulder. Ready to kill anything that threatened me. He had looked so steady. So sure of himself.

I was still trying to process it the next morning. That feeling of being saved. Something shifted inside of me. A childish crush became so much more. A boy saving a girl's life like that will change things. Don't you think?

Glancing at the river, I wondered if we were doing the right thing. What would happen to my chickens? Laughing I shook my head. They'd be eaten before the week was out. The only question, coyotes or people?

No, really, were we doing the right thing? Idaho was so far away. What if my family wasn't there? My grandfather would be. Nothing could make him leave his farm. He'd die before he left.

Once again a guilt filled me. I knew the only reason Luke had taken us away was because he felt responsible for keeping Sara and me alive. If he had his way he'd have stayed and fought it out.

Would we make it? It seemed so impossible. Looking at the saddles and packs put off to the side I did a mental inventory. I know, I know. One of my quirks. Two rifles, one shotgun, one pistol. At least two boxes of ammunition for each. Three for the shotgun. Forty pounds of oats. Ten pounds of dried dog food. A hundred pounds of food for us. Mostly beef jerky, smoked pork, and dried beans.

Not enough, I realized. We'd have to get more along the way.

How? We didn't have anything of value. Not in this new world.

A sound from the tent brought me back to reality. I couldn't help but smile as Luke stepped out. Shirtless, stretching and twisting.

I noticed a small scar on his lower back. Sara had told me years earlier that he'd gotten it by being bucked off a new bronc into a fence. He'd only been twelve and wasn't supposed to try and ride the horse. But he'd ignored everyone and ended up with a busted rib and an infected cut.

Two weeks later he'd ridden that horse. Now known by the name of Ajax.

He caught me staring at him and shot me a strange look. I felt my cheeks grow warm as I quickly looked away.

Letting out a long breath, he examined everything then smiled and nodded to me as he pulled on a shirt and marched off to the trees. When he came back he squatted down and started pulling things together to make a fire.

"I didn't know if I should," I told him. "People might see."

He pursed his lips and nodded. "I'm not sure. But we're going to be leaving right after breakfast. We can't get to Idaho without cooking along the way."

Nodding, I felt myself relax. This was so nice. Just Luke and I sharing a quiet morning.

"Thank you," I said suddenly. "For saving me. I never said thank you."

He shrugged as he held a lighter to the tinder then blew on it to get it going.

"And thank you for taking me to my family."

His forehead furrowed as he stared at me for a moment then said, "Cassie. It will be us thanking you. When we get there, for your family saving us."

"If we get there," I mumbled under my breath.

He froze for a moment then reached over to toss another stick on the fire. I noticed he didn't argue with me. No false bravado. No, that wasn't Luke. He was a realist. A cowboy who rode bulls had to look reality in the face. There was no pretending pain and suffering away.

After a quick breakfast of smoked bacon and cornmeal hush puppies cooked in the bacon grease, we were on our way. Again we stayed close to the river. We rode for about ten miles when we stopped for a noon meal and to give the horses a rest.

I noticed that Clancy dropped down in the shade, his tongue hanging out as he panted to cool off.

Sara was cooking some tortillas when I said to Luke, "Clancy, that is such a strange name for that type of dog. It sounds like he should be an Irish wolfhound or something. Why did you name him Clancy?"

He paused for a moment and I noticed the tips of his ears had turned red. Sara glanced at him, silently letting him know if he didn't tell me then she would. Of course my curiosity was reaching max.

Finally, he let out a long breath and said, "I didn't name him. Just after I turned fourteen, Dad let me work that summer with the Petersons."

I raised an eyebrow, asking for details.

Sara jumped in. "They raise rodeo stock, bulls, roping steers, Dad bought Cochise from them years ago."

Luke shrugged. "It was a cool job. Helping care for the animals. Moving them to and from the rodeos. They had a couple of Australian cattle dogs. I always admired the way they worked the stock. Tireless, never afraid. Smart as whips."

He looked off into the distance, remembering.

"Well one of theirs had a litter and I begged to have one of the puppies. Mom and Dad agreed but I had to convince the Peterson's. Actually their daughter, Julie. She was about six and loved those puppies. She'd named each of them."

Shooting me a quick smile he said, "She said the only way I could have one was if I agreed to keep his name. So. There you go."

I smiled to myself. Of course he hadn't gone back on his word and given the dog a more appropriate name. Not Luke Thompson.

A sad smile came over him as he shook his head. "I wonder how they are doing. The Peterson's. That little girl would be about ten now." He shuddered. The entire world was dying.

After a two-hour break, we hit the trail again. Twice we came across people camped along the river. Clancy always gave us a warning. Luke would lead us away from the river into the fields so we could work our way around them. Never getting within gunshot distance.

I could read Luke's mind. We had too much stuff. Even our horses could feed a family for six months.

A sickness filled me as I realized just how desperate people were going to get.

It was several hours before sunset when Luke pulled up in a bunch of trees a dozen yards from the river.

"Grass," He said as he pointed to a ditch running next to a field.

"But it is still light?"

He shook his head at me. "The horses shouldn't be pushed past twenty miles a day. Thirty if we have to."

I nodded. Twenty miles. It would take us months to get there. A doubt began to eat its way at my insides.

We set up a quick camp and settled in for the night. The trees broke up the smoke and the fire was hidden in a small gully. The three of us stared into the fire, each lost in our own thoughts. I knew Sara was thinking about the man she'd killed. I would see her looking off into the distance and just knew she was fighting to get rid of the images dancing in her head.

Luke didn't seem to have a care in the world. Of course, I knew him. He just wouldn't show it. He must feel the burden of being in charge. Always having to make decisions. Always being responsible.

My insides sort of melted. I had been so lucky. What of my brother Ryan? Had he made it to our grandfather's or was he lying dead beside some road? My father? A sadness hit me. Had he gotten away? Please I begged. Please be safe.

And my cousins, Haley, and Chase. They were just as important as Ryan to me. We'd grown up together. Haley was like my big sister. Always there for me. In New York City. My God. Could there be any place worse at the end of the world?

Phones. Our entire world revolved around phones. I could reach out and talk to my family at any time. Dad never would have let me visit Sara if he couldn't reach me at a moment's notice. But now. It was all gone.

Sadness threatened to overwhelm me when I pushed it away. No. I couldn't give in to it. Not now. Not here.

The afternoon turned to evening, the crickets came alive. The wind shifted ruffling the leaves. Finally, Luke started kicking dirt over the fire, telling us it was time to go to bed. Tomorrow was going to be a long day.

I almost laughed at myself. A month earlier I would have balked at being told what to do by this boy. Now it just seemed natural.

When I got into the tent I noticed Sara had taken the far side again. That meant I had the middle and Luke would be next to me. A small part of my soul screamed with happiness at the thought.

That night as I lay there fighting to get some sleep I thought about the boy next to me and wondered if he would ever see me as something other than his sister's best friend. As something other than a pest.

And if he did. How would Sara react?

Not well, I would bet.

A sad reality hit me as I realized I would never win this. First, Luke would never see me. Not the real me. And Sara would never forgive me if he did.

The next morning we cut across a field to a two-lane road.

"Why?" I asked Luke.

He nodded north, "We need to get to the Arkansas river. About twenty miles. We can't go just west."

A fear settled at the bottom of my stomach. The road was lined with telephone poles carrying now useless wires to the occasional farmhouse. We were so exposed up here on the road. Thankfully, it was nothing but flat fields for as far as the eye could see. The occasional line of trees for a wind break.

At noon we stopped at a crossroads. We had to water the horses from our canteens and let them on the grass down in the ditch.

That night when we got to the river we boiled water to refill our canteens then hunkered down.

"We'll follow this for a couple of days then head north again."

"The old Chism trail," I said with a smile.

His grin dropped as he shook his head. "Darn fences will keep us from following it too closely. This used to be prairie grass and sagebrush. We've turned it into corn and alfalfa fields. With more fences than not."

I smiled to myself. Luke would never think about cutting through the fences. The thought would never even cross his mind. He'd wrestled too much barbed wire to do that to another farmer.

Sara stood up to stretch then froze as she pointed in the distance.

Luke and I rose to see what she was pointing at. My heart fell when I saw the five men riding towards us.

Chapter Fourteen

Luke

I immediately pulled my rifle from my saddle's scabbard and made sure my pistol was still in its holster on my hip. I then told the girls to grab their guns and get down behind the lip of the small cliff next to the river.

Standing on the bluff, I waited for the men to approach. They weren't being sneaky. The smart thing would have been to get down behind the bluff with the girls but I was just too tired of backing down.

Besides the horses were up top.

My gut tightened as they approached. Youngish, twenties, they rode like they knew what they were doing. I gripped my rifle, ready. A thousand thoughts raced through my mind as I tried to anticipate all the bad things.

The men drew closer. The middle guy on a gray appaloosa pulled up and the others stopped forming a V. His eyes narrowed as he studied me for a moment then flicked over my shoulder to the two girls behind the bluff.

From the corner of my eye, I noticed a blond kid on a big roan smile when he saw the girls. Then lick his lips and reach over to nudge his partner in the ribs.

My gut tightened. I knew that look. That was an - I need some of that - look.

"Hello," I said to the middle guy.

His eyes narrowed then he said, "What you doing here? This is private property."

I scoffed then shook my head. "We're just passing through. We'll be gone in the morning."

He continued to frown as he slowly examined all of our supplies next to the saddles then the four horses picketed on the grass.

"Justin," one of the others said as he pointed to the girls. "We could take 'em in. Don't you think?"

A loud click behind me let me know Cassie had just chambered a round. You could have heard a mouse fart in church as the five men suddenly realized this wasn't playtime.

"They won't be going anywhere," I told them.

Suddenly Sara stood up, the shotgun level and steady. "Hey, we're right here. No need talking about us like we ain't. I've already killed one man with this. Who wants to be next?"

I couldn't stop from smiling as the color drained from their faces. The middle guy's brow furrowed then he said, "Be gone by the morning." He yanked on his horse's reins. Three others followed him but the blond continued to stare at Cassie with a look in his eyes that made my blood run cold.

An evil stare that let a person know exactly what he was thinking and it wasn't nice thoughts. About as far from nice as a man could get.

A need to just shoot him then and there flashed through me. But I held off. That small part of civilization hadn't been burned out of me just yet.

Seeing that his friends had left he turned around and followed them.

I swallowed and felt my fingers finally relax from where I'd been gripping my rifle. Standing there I watched them ride out of sight then turned to the girls and told them to start packing.

"What?"

"Why?"

"Just do it," I grumbled as I began saddling the horses. I knew what I had seen. Thirty minutes later after everything was ready Cassie was about to kick sand over the fire but I put a hand on her arm to stop her. Instead, I tossed two more large logs onto the fire.

She frowned at me. I could read it in her eyes. Leaving a fire unattended was wrong. Like cutting a fence. Just something you never did.

"We need for them to think we are still here. I want a dozen miles between us and them before they figure it out."

She continued to frown but Sara said, "He's right. That blond guy had a very dirty mind and I don't want him knowing we're on the road."

Cassie shrugged then climbed up on Cimarron. Sara had given her our mom's Lady's Stetson. Cassie pushed it down then looked at us as if asking what was taking us so long.

I laughed then led them down to the river. We rode through the water keeping the bluff between us and the horsemen.

The sun sank in the west and the air cooled as a nice breeze kissed us from the north. I made sure to put another five miles behind us before I found us a new campsite. It should be enough. They wouldn't know we were gone until the morning and by then it would be too late to follow.

We set up a quick camp and I told the girls no fire. We settled down for the night. Cassie next to me in her sleeping bag. Her rose shampoo crept into my soul as I turned over, away from her, searching for peace.

It was Clancy's low growl that woke me. Just loud enough for me. I was out of my bag and had my rifle cocked as I slowly lowered the zipper.

God, what a fool I had been. We were so vulnerable in a tent.

I hadn't gotten the zipper down when Clancy darted for the exit. I grabbed his collar and whispered, "No." I didn't want him charging off into the night. Not until I knew what we were facing.

Instead of standing up, I slithered out on my belly, crawling on my elbows like a snake, refusing to expose myself. Only when I'd gotten behind a large log did I lift up and study the night.

The half moon was out along with every star in a hazy sky. Ever since the asteroid the sky had a gauzy layer over everything. I could see two dozen yards. The silver light reflected off the bubbling river. The trees threw shadows and then I saw him. A man darting between trees.

Approaching our tent.

My gut tightened. If Clancy hadn't woken me. He would have killed us in our sleep. Slowly I lifted the rifle to my shoulder and took aim. It was the blond guy from earlier. Somehow he'd known we'd left then tracked us.

No, I realized. He hadn't tracked us. He'd simply followed the river. Another major mistake I thought as I mentally kicked myself.

Was he alone? What if the rest of them were hiding in the dark? If I shot, I'd give away my position. Swallowing hard, I forced myself to wait. The man darted to the next tree bringing himself within twenty yards of the tent.

I couldn't miss. One simple squeeze of the trigger and this man would die. The memory of the other two men I had killed danced through the front of my mind making me cringe inside. I didn't like the feeling.

But this man was threatening the girls. Even now they both slept, neither knowing how much danger they were in. Did I have the right not to kill this man where he stood?

I was still arguing with myself when he stepped out from the trees and hunched over as he crept closer.

Freezing, I took up the slack on the trigger and waited. Jesus the guy must be half blind. He hadn't seen me behind the log. Clancy lay next to me, as still as a fence post. He knew what was going on. No tail wags. No panting, just two eyes peeking above the log, every muscle ready to spring at the target if released.

The blond guy stopped just five feet from the tent and pulled a long knife from his belt. Then stepped closer, placing himself between me and the tent.

I didn't really think. I slowly stood up and brought the butt of my rifle to the back of his head. He dropped like a sack of potatoes.

The girls woke that morning to find him triced up with his hands tied behind his back, an egg-sized lump on the back of his head, and missing both his boots and his pants. I swear he blushed like a red beet when the girls saw him in his tighty whities.

Cassie raised an eyebrow at me.

"An unexpected caller," I told her then returned to feeding the fire. I wanted bacon.

We left him like that. Both girls looked at him, then at me, neither commented. Neither questioned my decision. I shot him a quick smile then said. "What's your name?"

He stared daggers at me then finally said, "Charles. Charles Stokes."

"Well Charley, I set your horse free. He's probably home by now. When your friends find him, I'll bet you donuts to dollars they don't come looking for you. You've got five miles to walk barefoot. And when you get there, you got to explain the whole no pants thing."

His face continued to grow even redder.

"Next time, I'll just shoot you when I see you."

He gulped then looked away, unwilling to admit he'd been bested. I nudged Ajax to a trot and forgot about him. He wouldn't be a problem.

We followed the Arkansas River for two more days. Where possible we tried to avoid people. When we moved up onto the road headed north I felt my gut tighten as I thought about those people who used to pass our farm.

That was us now. Refugees. And we were treated as such. Farmers would stand at their fence line with rifles ready making sure we moved along. I would dip my hat at them, letting them know we weren't a threat but they never relaxed. Not until we were gone.

The second night on the road we had to make a dry camp in a clump of trees between two fields. We had to be at least a mile from the nearest farmhouse but it was still too close so we made a fireless camp.

I had shifted to sleeping outside at night. I would set myself up in the shadows, Clancy next to me. Cassie had frowned that first night but neither she nor Sara questioned my decision. I just felt better. Besides I liked to fall asleep at night staring up at the stars. Trying to figure out what was going to happen next.

No matter what I thought about, I don't ever think I ever actually predicted things accurately.

We were a week into our quest when we crossed a major highway. A dozen cars were lying deader than doornails on the road. A reminder of how much we had lost. There were no planes in the sky. The railroad tracks on the other side of the highway would never be used again.

I thought about the thousand songs on my phone at home and felt a sadness settle over me. No music except what we made for ourselves and with my talent. That meant no music.

Taking a deep breath, I studied the road to make sure it was safe then waved the girls across. I pulled on Cochise's lead to get him going and got us across. A car had plowed through the barbed wire leaving a gap for us. But I held off. I knew the far side of the field would be fenced in. Instead, we rode along the side until we came to a north-running road and took a right.

We were about a mile from where I wanted to stop for the midday break when a farmer and his wife raced out of their house up their driveway to the road.

I cringed inside and made sure to put myself between the farmer and the girls. First thing I noticed was no rifle. Weird. I would never approach strangers again without a weapon. So yes, things had changed.

The man had to be sixty, his wife a few years younger. They weren't starving. Both were heavy set. Corn fed, we used to say. That Midwest farm spread.

"Morning," The man said, lifting his hand in greeting.

I glanced up at the sun. It was two hours past morning but I didn't say anything. Instead, I stopped Ajax and leaned forward on the saddle horn. "Hello."

He studied us for a minute, his eyes washing over the girls quickly. No lingering, longing looks. Especially not with his wife standing right there.

I was about to smile back when the woman glanced over her shoulder at the farmhouse, a worried look behind her eyes. Suddenly my alarms went off as I reassessed the situation. Lifting up, I looked around and noticed the place was surrounded by wire fence. No gate. That meant these weren't farmers.

No equipment shed. No silos. No chicken coup. What had these people been eating?

The man coughed. "We'd like to invite you' all to come up for dinner. We haven't had many visitors. Where you lot from?"

I continued to examine the man and his wife. Something just didn't fit. I couldn't put my finger on it but I'd learned to listen to that feeling. It was like getting on a bull that had your name. You just knew it was going to end up with you lying in the dirt.

Glancing over at the girls I noticed Cassie was feeling it too. She gave me a subtle shake of her head.

"Sorry," I told the couple. "We've got to put more distance for the day. Can't stop."

The look of disappointment in their eyes told me I'd made the right decision. It wasn't the disappointment of missing good things. It was the disappointment of fear.

I clicked my tongue to get Ajax moving. The girls followed. Suddenly I saw movement coming out of the house. Two men with rifles.

"Ya," I yelled as I spurred my horse. The girls saw it too and were right with me. We were two hundred yards down the road before the men slid out from the driveway. I leaned forward expecting a bullet to slam into my back but we were just too far away for them to waste ammunition.

When we were two miles down the road I pulled Ajax to a trot then a walk and asked the girls if they were okay.

"What was that all about?" Cassie asked as she looked over her shoulder. Her chest rose as she gulped in air.

"I think they were going to get us inside and kill us. We were too out in the open to attack us straight up. So get us inside and take us there."

Cassie shook her head. "Is everyone going to try to kill us?"

I shrugged my shoulders. "Not everyone. But enough so that you've got to assume the worst."

Her eyes grew misty as she looked to the north. I could read the thoughts dancing through her mind. How could we ever make Idaho if everyone between here and there was going to try to kill us?

Chapter Fifteen

Northern Idaho

On a small farm in Northern Idaho, a young man named Ryan Conrad stepped out onto the porch and stared to the south. "Cassie. Where are you?" he whispered.

Haley and Chase had both made it to the farm. Dad had said he wasn't supposed to go down there and get Cassie from Oklahoma. They'd miss each other on the road. But a deep doubt ate at his insides. She was his little sister. His responsibility.

Glancing down he sighed, his last cup of coffee. They'd checked in town last week. No one had coffee to trade.

That permanent anger nipped at his gut. It never went away, the problems. They never went away. Cassie being a thousand miles away was just the worst of them.

Sighing, he took a long sip then glanced over at the fields and smiled softly. They'd done it. Put in three acres of corn and three more of potatoes. Keley's Mom had coordinated four different gardens. They should have enough to get through the winter.

Glancing up at the sky he shuddered. The air had been hazy, filled with dust for the last two months. Would it affect the crops?

Nobody knew anything. This was all new territory. They said the dinosaurs died out because of the dust and dirt thrown up by their asteroid killer. Was there's that bad?

The screen door closed behind him and he felt Kelsey come up behind him and wrap her arms around his waist while she buried her head on his back. "You're thinking about going to get Cassie, aren't you?"

Sighing, he shrugged. Three months together and she could read him like a book. "It'd take us three months to get down there. Three more to get back. It'd be the dead of winter. And these mountains aren't very friendly in the winter."

"Us?" she asked.

"Chase and I have been talking."

There was a long silence then she pulled back and turned him around, staring up into his eyes. "I understand. She is your sister. You helped me find my mom. We never would have found each other without you."

He nodded, "But?"

She smiled sadly. "We've done so much. Chase and Meagan have converted the loft in the barn. Haley and Tanner have their room with the baby."

Ryan's heart hitched when she hesitated about the baby Haley had rescued. She did that a lot lately. Did she disagree with them bringing the baby with them?

"What is it?" he asked.

She took a deep breath and held it for a long moment. "You have every right to go. I shouldn't do anything to stop you."

"You could come with us," he said then immediately regretted it. No way was he putting her in that much danger.

She looked up into his eyes then pulled him close so she could lay her head on his chest. "I can't."

"Can't, not won't?"

There was a long hesitant pause then she said, "I wasn't going to tell you. I didn't want to influence your decision. But ... But if something happened..." Here she hesitated again, both of them had seen so much death along the road to the farm. Both knew what she was saying."

Pulling back she stared up at him. "But I didn't want you leaving without knowing that I'm pregnant."

He froze as his world adjusted to this new reality. "Are you sure? How?"

She laughed then slugged him in the arm. "I am not explaining the birds and bees to you, Mr. Conrad."

He pulled her into a deep hug and let the idea of being a father wash over him. This was so unbelievable. Yet so right. He loved this woman with all his heart. He would die to protect her. And now the baby. No, this was how things were supposed to be.

"This changes things," he whispered.

"Are you upset at me?" she asked without looking at him.

He chuckled then held her tighter. "I love you more every day."

"I'm going to get so fat."

Again he laughed and said. "You know perfectly well that you will be a beautiful mother. And you will do such a good job. Does your mom know?"

She nodded into his chest then said, "I don't want to stop you from going. But I wanted you to know."

Sighing, he turned to look south. His woman was pregnant with his child. How could he leave her? Yet his sister was somewhere between the farm and Oklahoma. Had they even left? Maybe she was safer where she was. Had Dad told her to leave and come to the farm or had he told her to stay there. It was probably smarter to stay in one spot.

A deep doubt hit him. Either way, he would be making the wrong decision. Abandoning Kelsey, or Cassie.

For the thousandth time, he cursed the asteroid and the damage it had left behind. Only months ago he could have boarded a plane gone down there and got her and been home by the next day.

Or he could have talked with his sister and coordinated a rescue. Discovered if she even needed to be rescued.

But now. Ever since that damn rock had fallen from the sky, the world had become too unfair.

"What do you think?" Kelsey asked hesitantly, "Are you going to go?"

He looked south, then down at his love, and shrugged. "I don't know."

A small tear formed in the corner of her eye before spilling over and trickling down her cheek. Sniffling she wiped at it and said, "Don't mind me. I get emotional for no reason. The baby."

He smiled at her then looked south. What should he do? What was the right move?

Chapter Sixteen

Cassie

I spent that morning looking north and wondering about my brother. Had he made the farm? Was he dead in some ditch, dying alone? Or had he been trapped in Seattle and killed by the tsunami? Would I ever know the truth?

And Haley, Chase, my dad. Were any of them alive? Was I the last Conrad? Had a vibrant, valuable family been erased from Earth's history? A sadness bit at me as I fought to hold the depression off.

The world just plain sucked. And always would. Especially now.

We continued working our way north. Luke continued to not see me. Not as a girl. No, I would always be Sara's little friend.

An anger bubbled deep inside of me. I was angry at so many things. Luke, for being Luke. Sara for never understanding and not even knowing what she was doing to me. I was angry at the world for dying. Angry at my family for not being safe. Furious at the people we met along the way.

They were either taking from others, or cowering, waiting for someone to come by and save them.

The anger turned over to sadness as I thought about the family we had seen the day before. They looked like they'd been on the road for a month. Mainly because they had been. Living off handouts and what they could glean from the fields.

Dried corn kernels left by the combines.

All four of them looked skinnier than fence rails. Torn clothes, dirty faces, hands cracked and scarred, embedded with soil. My heart broke seeing the little girl looking up at me with sunken eyes. The eyes of a person without much to live for.

We'd come up on them headed north along a deserted farm road. "Luke," I hissed when I saw the hunger in their eyes.

He sighed heavily then reached into his saddlebags and pulled out a pack of beef jerky wrapped in plastic and tossed it to the father.

The man caught it in mid-air while never taking his eyes off Luke. I could read it all there, Why were we so lucky? Why did we get to have horses, food, guns? All while his family struggled to stay alive.

No pleas for more. No thank you. Just an angry stare. This was a man fighting the demons of failure. He was supposed to provide and protect his family. But he was failing. His wife stood next to him in a flimsy cotton dress and shoes with broken soles.

My heart broke. That could be us if we lost the horses.

Luke grumbled deep in his throat then nudged his horse to hurry. The sooner we were away from those people the sooner we could relax. The sooner we could stop feeling guilty.

That was something I had learned. The sense of guilt did not last. There were too many things to go wrong. We were too close to stepping off the survival wagon and into despair.

A few miles later Luke pointed to a sign saying we were entering Kansas.

Sara scoffed and shook her head and turned to Luke. "Remember that trip to Virginia. We'd always celebrate every time we would cross over into a new state. Mom always made a big deal about it."

The sadness in her eyes tore at my soul. That wound had not healed. It never would, not fully.

We worked our way out of the farm country into a more open plain. Land too dry and too barren for crops. Just clumps of brown grass and sagebrush with distant cows. Two days later we were back into farm country. I glanced over to find Luke shaking his head.

"More farms,"

My heart fell. We preferred the open countryside, away from people. The thought made me chuckle to myself. Farms a mile apart and that was too many people.

Sighing heavily, I followed Sara and Luke down the road. That became our life. Weaving through farms, staying close to rivers and creeks where possible. Avoiding towns at all costs.

We'd find a hidden gully or creek bed to camp at night. Luke would sleep outside under the stars with Clancy. And yes, I was a bit jealous of the dog. The days just blended together. All the while a deep worry behind everything. Would we make it? What would we find when we got there? And then what? How did the world survive without electricity?

Every night became a routine. We'd unsaddle the horses and wipe them down. Luke would check their hooves to make sure they hadn't picked up a stone. I knew deep down that he was particularly worried about losing the horses. Even losing one could ruin our chances.

Once they'd settled down, he'd give them a hatful of oats or turn them out on fresh grass.

While he worked with the horse, Sara and I would set up the tent, get a fire going then someone would cook a quick meal.

Beans and tortillas sprinkled with pemican. Once a week we'd open a can of peaches and make a cobbler.

If we were close to water we'd try fishing. If we were lucky the fish would be saved for our breakfast. Then we were on the road again.

It became a bit boring. At least until I caught Luke unpacking all of our food. I saw how little we had left and felt a cold chill rush down my spine.

"We're going to have to stop somewhere. Work for some cornmeal at least."

Sara frowned, "We could trade."

"What?" Luke scoffed.

"Momma's jewelry,"

"Sara?" Luke gasped. "Did you bring it? No, we can't do that."

"Oh, Luke, she won't care. I'll keep grandma's wedding ring. But the rest. She doesn't mind. I promise you."

I tightened my lips and kept out of it. This was between them. But I agreed with Sara. It was only gold and silver. You couldn't eat gold and silver.

Two days later we walked the horses into the town of Bourne. A small farming town, little more than a village, with a John

Deere dealership on main street between a supermarket and a church. A big brick library across the street. Wide sidewalks, a now useless stoplight above the only intersection.

No barriers stopping us from coming in. The people looked sullen but they weren't starving. I remembered that family on the road and prayed they made it this far. If I was them and I got to this town I would never leave.

The streets were clear. The stalled cars had been pushed to the side. There were horse dropping in the middle of the street so we weren't the only ones shifting back to the old ways.

We stopped in front of the darkened supermarket. Luke swung down from his horse and handed Sara his reins.

"No," she said as she passed them over to me. "You wouldn't know what anything is worth." Rummaging through her saddlebags, she retrieved a small cloth bag and gave me a sad smile.

Twenty minutes later she and Luke returned with a ten-pound bag of flour and four boxes of cornmeal.

"That is it?" I gasped.

Sara's cheeks turned red.

Luke patted her on the shoulder. "Don't worry about it, Sis. You couldn't shift them. They've got the food. They've got the power to say no."

My stomach curled in on itself as I realized how little we had to go so far.

We ended up making it all the way across the Colorado corner. We'd just crossed over into Wyoming when the last of it ran out.

"This time It's my turn," Luke said as we worked our way into another small town. This was only the second time we'd been around civilization since leaving. It was three months after the asteroid hit. Mid-summer in Wyoming, not the easiest place to be.

Fewer people and more cows. Twice we came across barriers manned by men with guns. We never argued but pulled back and worked our way around. That was the thing about the mid-west. There was just too much land to block it all.

I had noticed some changes. Fewer people on the road. My stomach would turn over on itself every time I thought about it. People were dying off, I realized. That was why. I thought about that family of four. Had they made it to Bourne? And if they had, had the town taken them in or forced them to keep moving?

Luke pointed to the far distance. "Bureau of Land Management land. No fences. Or not as many."

I laughed and looked out at the rolling hills of brown clumps of grass between sage bushes. The hazy sky didn't stop the sun from trying to bake us to a crisp. Both Sara and I were torn between putting our hair up to catch a breeze or keeping it down to protect our necks from sunburn.

We moved off the road. Clancy racing ahead to scope out our route. He had held up well, I thought to myself. But we weren't pushing the horses. We'd only gone about halfway so far. No, protecting them was our number one priority.

I marveled at Clancy's endurance then thought of those sled dogs in Alaska running for days. Or wolves running down an elk or buffalo. No, he was designed for this.

We were two days into Wyoming when Luke suddenly pulled up as the color drained from his face. My heart raced as I turned to follow his stare. A wall of black clouds was creeping up from behind us.

I'd seen clouds like that before. Hell, every kid who grew up in Oklahoma knew tornado clouds when she saw them.

Twisting around, I realized just how exposed we were. There wasn't a building for five miles in any direction.

Luke stood up in his stirrups then pointed before yelling and spurring Ajax. The horse hopped then tore into the ground, racing through the sage. Cimarron hated being left behind and Brandy wasn't much better. Within seconds we were all running across the prairie.

Where? I wondered. What was his plan? I knew Luke, he'd save us. He always did. And what if one of the horses tripped. We'd be trapped out here in the open.

Looking over my shoulder, I cringed inside, The storm was moving faster than us. Faster than a galloping horse. Swallowing hard I stared, searching for a long tendril of twirling air.

Lightning flickered followed seconds later by the boom of thunder shaking the ground louder than the pounding hooves of our horses. Then I saw it. The gulch up ahead. Luke was leaning over his horse's neck, holding Cochise's lead, looking back to make sure Sara and I were with him.

We almost made it but came up a hundred yards short. The skies opened up and it was like being dunked in a pool. The day grew dark. One moment it was light then it wasn't. One moment a cool wind was tickling our backs the next a thousand buckets of water were dumped on us.

The only thing that saved us was the absence of a tornado. A thunderstorm can be survived. A twister not so much. Not out on the open plain.

Ignoring the water and wind, I followed Luke down into the gulch. Maybe six feet deep. A flash flood stream dryer than dryer lint. At least for the moment.

Luke was off his horse before he stopped, reaching back for the pack horse, whispering in their ears, calming them just as a lightning bolt exploded a hundred yards up the gulch rocking the world with thunder.

Another shaft of lightning rose up from the prairie, followed almost immediately by a clap of thunder that made me cringe and duck, positive hell had opened up. The sharp tang of brimstone biting the back of my throat.

My stomach clenched tight as we hid down there in the gulch while the rain washed over us. The wind bounced over our heads. Clancy wove his way between Luke and the gully wall. We fought to keep the horses calm. Praying it would end quickly. Praying we weren't hit by a tornado.

I told myself to ignore the rain. Just be glad it wasn't hail. It was just like swimming. I was too wet to worry about it. Finally, the rain let up then passed on like all summer storms. All bark and no lasting bite.

Letting out a long sigh I looked to up find Luke staring at me, his eyes wide in shock. "What?" I said, frowning.

He continued to stare at me, his eyes traveling up and down my body. I didn't mind but I couldn't understand then suddenly Sara reached into her bag and tossed me her flannel shirt. I was still trying to work it out when I looked down and realized I was wearing a white T-shirt. Because of the water, Luke could see everything.

And he'd liked what he saw. I was positive of that. I'd seen it in his eyes. I wasn't his sister's little friend. Not when I was standing there soaked to the skin. Not when he could see everything worth seeing.

I will admit to taking a little time putting on Sara's shirt over the top. I will also admit to being disappointed when Luke turned away from me to see to his horses. I'd liked seeing that hungry look in his eyes. A girl could live off this feeling for months.

Chapter Seventeen

Luke

You know how there are certain images, pictures, that bounce around in your brain? You can't get rid of them no matter how hard you try. The more you want to erase them the more they stay. Especially the images that you don't really want to forget.

That was the image of Cassie in her wet T-shirt. An image that changed everything. She stopped being Sara's best friend in that instant. At least in my mind. And yes, I knew she was off limits. Out of bounds. Untouchable. Why do you think I wanted to get rid of that image?

Because as long as that was all I saw whenever I thought about her. Then I was going to be fighting with myself on a constant basis.

We spent every moment of every day together. And just when I thought I might be able to put the image aside I would find her bent over the fire. Or smiling kindly at Cimarron. Or I'd catch a hint of rose shampoo.

And once more, my mind would be filled with that image.

"Luke!" Sara snapped, giving me a strange look.

"What?" I stammered as I fought to not blush. If my sister discovered what I was thinking about Cassie she'd never talk to me again.

Sara's brow furrowed then she took a deep breath and pointed ahead. I'd been so lost in my own thoughts I hadn't seen us approaching a small town. "I saw it," I lied. "We need to stop and see if we can find food.

Both girls continued to look at me with doubt. I could swear Sara knew I was lying but she chose not to challenge me about it.

Get your head in the game, I told myself as I adjusted the gun on my hip and made sure my rifle would slide out of its scabbard easily. We approached the town slowly, expecting the worst. We'd taken care to avoid towns ever since leaving home, riding miles out of our way if necessary.

But we needed stuff.

The first thing I noticed was the absence of barriers. At least half the towns we came close to had some kind of barrier up. Cars pushed into position to block the road. In one town they'd unloaded two dozen hay bales. But this town was open.

The second thing I noticed was the dead body lying in the gutter.

Sara gasped as Brandy shied away.

Holding up a hand, I stopped us as I studied the body. A man in his forties. A farmer's John Deere hat, on his back staring up at the sky. He looked fresh. The birds and ants hadn't gotten to him yet.

"What happened to him?" Cassie asked.

I was about to give her a snarky answer when I bit my tongue. Again one of those changes. Pretty girls are treated differently. And ever since that rain storm Cassie had been moved into the top category when it came to prettiness.

Instead, I shook my head then looked up into the town. One main street, businesses, houses behind them. Two intersections with dead traffic lights. But no people.

Sara coughed, "I don't like this."

My gut was telling me that she was right. I was about to pull Ajax around when a door slammed. A woman of about sixty walked out into the street, holding her hand up to shield her eyes as she studied us.

"What's going on?" I asked as I pointed to the dead body.

She continued to study us for a minute then said, "Typhoid. Either that or cholera. I can't tell the difference. Half the town is sick. The other half is waiting to get sick."

My stomach tightened. Of all the stupid towns in this godforsaken state and we walked into the one with Typhoid. I didn't ask more questions. I didn't discuss it with the girls. Instead, I wheeled Ajax around and pulled at Cochise's lead. "Let's go."

Both girls shot me worried frowns then followed me out of the town and back down the road we had come in on. I made sure we gave that town a three-mile berth and worked our way around. The girls were quiet, shooting me concerned looks.

Finally, Cassie couldn't wait any longer, "Do we need to be worried? Can we catch it?"

Letting out a long breath, I shook my head. "I think both Cholera and Typhoid are passed in the water."

"But how'd they get it?" Sara asked.

"Sanitation," I told them. "If you think about it, plumbers save more lives than doctors."

"But ... I mean how?" Sara continued.

"Outhouses. The waste gets into the groundwater. Wells get contaminated. I don't know. But without medicines. I bet it spread pretty fast. Plus, nobody has been exposed to those germs in a hundred years. Their natural immunity has got to be crap."

Both girls grew silent. I could tell their minds were running a million miles a second. Not only did they have to worry about bandits on the road. But now they had to worry about minuscule germs they couldn't even see until it was too late.

"The next town we hit. We need to see if we can get some Clorox. Purify the water. Otherwise, we make sure to boil it for ten minutes. Maybe both. Just to be sure."

We continued on and found a creek about fifteen miles past the town to bed down for the night. As I lay there staring up at the stars. That damn image popped back into my head. The picture of Cassie that refused to leave me alone. At the exact same time, I heard her sigh heavily in the tent then turn over.

She was only six feet away. God, a man could be driven crazy.

It took us two more days to find another town. Again, just like the others we'd passed, a gathering place for ranchers and farmers. Two bars, three churches, a small grocery store, and odds and ends. Two dozen homes.

They'd somehow wrestled cement jersey barriers into place to block the one street into town. An old man sat in a lawn chair with a shotgun across his lap. He didn't get up as we approached. Instead, he looked up and said. "Can't come through."

"We wanted to see about trading?" I said to him as I leaned to rest on the saddle horn.

He studied us and I could see his mind working out the details. Horses well cared for. Hats and boots. Comfortable in the saddle. We weren't city people. His brow narrowed as he asked, "What you got?"

I smiled, now I had him. "We want to talk to the people in charge of the grocery store."

He laughed then shrugged. "Good luck, they got themselves killed the third day. The idiot manager was new. From out of town. Thought he was in charge. He learned different."

Nodding I said, "We're looking for food. Flour mostly. Corn meal."

He tilted his head and studied us. "I got ten pounds of flour I might want to trade. We divvied up the grocery store on the fourth day. Fair share each. But I don't go through food too fast. What you got?"

Shrugging I said nodding to his weapon, "A box of 12-gauge shotgun shells."

He laughed. "Boy, this is Wyoming. We've got more ammunition than the Army."

My heart dropped. We didn't have anything else. At least he hadn't looked at the girls. Not in a wanting-to-take kind of way. Sighing heavily I shrugged my shoulders and turned to leave.

"Hold on boy," the man yelled from behind us. "We was just getting started and you're already giving up?"

I shrugged, stopping my turn but not turning back, waiting. It was his move.

"I don't need shotgun shells," he said as he lifted his weapon. "But is that a .44 I see on your hip. A magnum?"

Nodding, I waited.

"I know a man. Got himself a magnum. But he used up a lot of his ammo that first week. He'd be willing to give me a good bit for a box of shells."

"No," I said as I continued my turn. Both girls frowned at me. "Not for just a bag of flour. That's too much."

He smiled slightly then said, "I'll throw in ten pounds of beef, slaughtered yesterday. Cows we got plenty of."

"And ..." I asked.

He thought for a minute then said, "How about I add four boxes of macaroni and cheese."

My heart fell as I realized what I was giving up for some food. But really we didn't have a choice. He was right. There was a lot of ammunition available. We'd lucked into a good situation. Of course it was three days before I realized we didn't have butter or milk for the powdered cheese.

"Okay," I said. "Throw in a bottle of Clorox. I'm sure you've got some. We'll wait here. You get the stuff."

Twenty minutes later we were on the road. We gorged ourselves on roast steaks that night and all of the next day making sure the meat was eaten before it could go bad. That hot Wyoming sun didn't give us much time.

We continued north, avoiding people where we could. But sometimes it was just impossible. Bridges across rivers, roads up through mountains. Farms we had to cross. The land had become more bare. Harder, more ranch than farm, if you know what I mean.

It was a normal morning. Hazy. Always hazy. With a small western wind tugging at the sagebrush. It must have been about ten, two hours before we would stop to give the horses a rest. Suddenly Clancy turned and started barking.

I looked over my shoulder and felt my gut clench. Riders, three of them raced across the prairie directly toward us. We didn't have time to find out if they were friendly or not. "Go," I yelled as I spurred Ajax.

Both girls yelled at their horses and we were off, racing across the prairie, weaving through sagebrush, over ditches, and around rocky outcroppings. Clancy racing to keep up.

My stomach tightened when I realized they were gaining on us. "Go boy," I urged as I leaned forward. But we were too heavily loaded. Between the camping gear, the food. Plus the horses had been pushed for six weeks on little feed. Not the good kind.

We weren't going to make it. I pulled back slightly and let the girls catch up. "Here," I yelled as I passed Cochise's lead to Cassie then slapped his butt to keep him going.

"What ..." She yelled over her shoulder all the while we continued to gallop across the ground.

"Go," I yelled then wheeled Ajax around as I pulled my rifle from its scabbard. And tugged him to a stop. The men were getting closer. Maybe two hundred yards. I hadn't even lifted my rifle when a shot rang out and I felt the buzz of a bullet over my left shoulder.

I didn't wait, I didn't think, I squeezed my knees into Ajax to steady him then slowly pulled the trigger. The man on the right yelled then swerved out of pursuit. Immediately I swung to the middle man and fired but I missed.

The two remaining men began firing as they continued to race towards me. For some reason, I thought about being charged by a grizzly bear. This must be what it felt like. I couldn't turn and run. They'd have me for sure. I had to stand there and face them.

Taking a calming breath, I forced my heart to stop pounding in my chest as I took careful aim and fired. The lead horse stumbled. My heart dropped, had I missed the man and hit the horse? But before I could refocus a burning pain along my side brought me back to reality.

I'd been hit. How bad I didn't know. But I didn't have time. The one remaining man hadn't stopped. Who was this guy? Why didn't he break off? He'd closed the distance to less than a hundred yards. He fired again.

I ignored the buzz past my cheek and focused. This might be my last chance. This time I aimed for center mass and fired.

The man threw his hands up and fell off the back of his horse. I'd hit him. In fact, I was pretty sure I'd killed the man. Once again I was filled with guilt and doubt but I pushed it aside. I needed to find the girls.

As I turned Ajax I felt a burn in my side. Looking down I discovered my shirt was red with blood and I felt a weakness fill me as the world grew a little wobbly.

Chapter Eighteen

Cassie

I held my breath as Sara and I waited for Luke. We'd stopped at a line of trees serving as a windbreak along a drainage ditch with puddles of water between two farms. I watched in the far distance as Luke calmly fired, first at one man, then another and his horse. And finally, the third man fell.

My soul soared to new heights as I realized Luke would live then dropped like a brick when I realized that once again we had to kill to survive. But then I realized he was alive. Anything was justified.

Smiling from ear to ear, I watched him calmly turn Ajax and start for us. The boy was a born hero. He'd just saved us and he acted all cool and calm. Like he did this every day.

I swear my heart melted, pure and simple. Melted.

"Your brother," I said to Sara, shaking my head.

She shot me a strange look but she didn't disagree.

We waited in the shade then I saw Luke bend forward, holding his side. I held my breath until I saw the red stain on his lower left side.

"What?" I yelped as I jumped down to race to his side just as he started to fall out of the saddle. Reaching up, I caught him, just enough to break his fall and gently lay him down. My world stopped as I looked down at the blood on my hands. Suddenly the truth hit me. Luke was hurt. Bad hurt.

"No," I yelled as I dropped to my knees then yelled for Sara, "Get the first aid kit. It's on Cochise's pack."

"Luke," I said to him as I gently cupped his face, smearing it with his own blood on my hands, "you're hurt."

He scoffed and lifted one eyelid. "You think?"

Those two words soothed my soul. He wasn't going to die. I wouldn't let it happen. No.

I was going to ask him where but realized it was sort of obvious. The long tear in his shirt sort of pointed the way. I pulled his knife from his sheath and cut away his shirt. My heart fell when I saw the jagged cut along his side.

"It doesn't look like it hit anything," Sara said as she dropped down on the other side then opened the first aid kit next to her.

I grabbed bandages and told her to start a fire to boil water. "We're going to have to use our drinking water to clean the wound." So that was what we did. I cleaned away the blood before covering the wound in gauze then Sara and I wrapped him in ace bandages to hold the gauze in place.

When we were done, I stared down at him, terrified. What would I do if he died? My life would be over. Not just getting to my grandfather's but my reason for living. "Please," I whispered as I pushed the hair out of his eyes.

"Let's get him under the trees," Sara said.

All I could do was nod. We gently rolled him onto a blanket and dragged him in under the trees. I immediately dropped down to check on him, terrified we'd opened up his wound again. Maybe we should have waited.

He didn't respond. Just lay there taking shallow breaths. I reached out to gently touch his shoulder, unable not to. I didn't worry about Sara seeing how much I cared. All I could think about was not losing him.

Sometime later Sara joined me then gently told me to go rest.

I turned to find that she'd seen to the horses, set up the tent, and had a small fire going. How had I missed all of that? "I can't."

She frowned softly then let out a long sigh. "Get some rest. We're going to have to trade off through the night."

I glanced at the setting sun and realized we'd been there for two hours already. I looked back down at him then back across the fields. He'd killed that third man for sure. If the shot hadn't done it, then falling off that horse that way had. But what about the other men? Did we need to fear them?

Glancing over, I saw that Clancy had his head up, focused back towards our attackers. My insides relaxed but I made a point of grabbing the rifle from my saddle and telling Sara I was going to make a round.

She frowned up at me then nodded.

Tapping my leg for Clancy I walked out into the field about fifty yards then made a long circle around our camp. What would Luke do? I kept asking myself. What would he look for? I had absolutely no idea and kicked myself for never asking.

But as I walked I told myself that regardless, nothing was allowed to hurt Luke ever again. Not when I was around. So eventually we finished the round.

"Is it all clear?" Sara asked.

"Clancy says it is," I told her as I looked down at Luke.

The two of us sat next to him, neither wanting to admit how scared we were. Sara took a deep breath then smiled sadly, "Don't worry," she said, "He has been stomped by bulls, got knocked cold on the football field more than once. And they had a running tab at the emergency room. Nothing can hurt Luke."

I cringed inside when I saw the fear in her eyes. This was her big brother. The only family she had left. Without thinking I reached out to take her hand. We sat there like that until the sun went down.

Neither of us was going to leave his side. Not until we knew he would be alright. One of us would occasionally get up to feed the fire. Another would check the wounds. The bleeding had stopped.

We'd removed his shirt and had him covered in two blankets. I was bent over checking the bandage when he suddenly grabbed my wrist. "Stop," he croaked. "The blood's dry. You keep pulling it."

My insides froze with anger at myself. How could I be so stupid? I was hurting him. Hurting my Luke. I swear, I don't think I had ever felt a greater sense of guilt and shame all rolled into one. All mixed with relief that he was awake.

"Luke," Sara said coming back from the fire.

He smiled up at his sister then whispered, "Water."

My insides relaxed he was going to be okay, I just knew it.

We fussed over him until he pushed us away and tried to sit up. The blanket fell away from that broad chest.

"Hold on," I said as I put my hand on his shoulder to keep him down.

He stared at me, daring me to try and stop him. I swear it was like a wolf staring into your soul. A man that was not to be denied. Swallowing hard, I pulled my hand away.

"Help me up," he grumbled as he got to all fours. Both Sara and I helped him stand, both of us holding on to him as he swayed back and forth. Finally, he stabilized himself then pushed our hands away and started for the bushes.

I stepped next to him ready to catch him if he fell.

"Back off, Cassie," he snapped, shooting me that stare again.

"Why are you mad at me," I snapped back at him.

He rolled his eyes. "Because I want to go to the bathroom alone."

Gulping I stopped and let him go into the bushes. He leaned against a tree then came back out and sighed heavily. "We need to move."

"Move?" Both Sara and I said at the same time. "Are you crazy? You can't go anywhere."

He grit his jaw then leaned down and picked up a blanket to start folding it.

"Luke," I said as I gently touched his arm. "You need to rest."

"We need to go before they find us," he said through gritted teeth. "We're too close. I didn't kill them all." The look of regret in his eyes shocked me. Three months ago, the thought of killing a man would have tormented his soul for the rest of his life. Now, he regretted not finishing the job.

"Sit," Sara said, "Before you fall over. Cassie and I will pack the horses. You just sit and wait."

Thirty minutes later I was kicking sand over the fire. We'd both helped Luke up onto his horse then joined him on ours. I took Cochise's lead, Sara led the way out of the camp. Luke in the middle where I could keep an eye on him.

We followed a dirt track to a gravel road then followed it until we hit pavement.

"South," Luke said. He was using both hands around the horn to stay in his saddle. "We were headed north when they came at us. Now that we can ride without leaving tracks. Go south, three miles at least."

That would put us ten miles from where we were attacked. Was that enough distance? But we couldn't push the horses too much and I could see in the silver moonlight that Luke was turning pale. The sooner we stopped the better.

We made a cold camp next to a creek behind a bluff. It took both Sara and I to get Luke down off his horse. He more fell than a smooth transition. We got him on a blanket next to the bluff then took care of the horses and set up the camp.

"You watch him first," Sara said. "I'll grab some sleep. Wake me in two hours."

I nodded and started towards him but she grabbed my arm and pulled me back. "Two hours. If you don't then I will know you're in love with him."

"Sara," I gasped.

She just stared at me then said, "Two hours."

I watched her crawl into the tent then hurried to Luke's side. The moon was about to set so I used the last of its light to orient myself and check on him. The bandage was slightly red from new blood but it looked like it had stopped again.

He was out. Sleeping.

Sitting down I gently touched his arm. Unable to not touch him. Was Sara right? Was I in love with Luke Thompson?

No, impossible. It was one of those stressful danger things. Throw two people together in stressful situations and they would get feelings. It was normal, right?

"No," I whispered to myself. One thing I knew without doubt. Luke did not feel anything like this for me. Besides, Sara would hate me forever if she thought I was into her brother. That was the unbreakable rule between best friends.

No, I couldn't be in love with Luke. The starlight let me study him and my heart melted. Who was I kidding? Of course, I was in love with him. The boy was every girl's dream. Cute, Manley to the tenth degree but without being harsh or mean.

I looked over at Clancy on his other side and smiled to myself. A boy with a cool dog who thought his master walked on water. No, a dog like Clancy couldn't be wrong. But there was something more. Some magic that pulled me to him.

His confidence. The way nothing seemed to ruffle him. Smart without being a know-it-all.

That was it, I realized. Why I loved him. It was all the stuff, but most of all it was the way he treated me. Yes, I was his little sister's best friend. But he'd never treated me like I was stupid, or worthless.

Closing my eyes, I pushed back the tears. I was a hopeless case. I'd fallen in love with a boy who could never love me back. The world was ending and I'd chosen the worst situation possible to make it more horrific.

A tear spilled out from the corner of my eye as my heart broke. I swear I don't know if I could have been more unhappy and I don't know what I would have done if he hadn't whispered, "Cassie,"

I froze.

"Cassie," he said again as he twisted in his sleep.

He was calling my name. In his sleep. Suddenly my world didn't seem so terrible. Suddenly there was the faintest of hope. Just enough to keep a girl in the game.

Chapter Nineteen

Luke

My side burned and my head felt like they were building a road through the middle of it. But I'd survive. Unlike some of those men, I'd shot the day before.

I waited for the anguish, the shame to hit me. Killing wasn't right. We weren't monsters. But deep down I knew the truth. It was them or us. Simple. Did that excuse it? I thought for a moment then scoffed. Yes, it did. If they hadn't come racing at us, shooting, trying to get us to stop.

No, the girls deserved to live free and unharmed. Of course I was right to shoot those men. And with that, I told myself I would never think of them again.

Sighing, I laid back down and held up a hand to block the sun. Cassie saw it and scurried to hang a blanket to give me some shade. I could only smile and shake my head. The girl was hovering. "I'm fine," I told her. "I've been worse."

She forced a smile then turned to tidy up around camp. She's nervous, I realized. Why? No way did she think I was that sick. Was she nervous about us staying in the area? We'd talked it through. The horses needed a good day of rest. I sort of could use an easy day also. There was water, good grass. A bluff to block anyone seeing a fire. Trees to hide the smoke. It was perfect. So why was she nervous?

I swear she was folding that blanket for the third time. She suddenly froze then rushed to the gear Cochise normally carried. She dug around then squealed with delight as she pulled a small bag and hurried back to me. Smiling from ear to ear she removed three pills and handed them out for me.

"The painkillers and anti-biotics you traded for. Remember. I should have given them to you last night."

I looked at the pills in her hand and felt my insides relaxed. I'd been worried about an infection. And the painkillers would help me get back on the road even faster. Looking up at her I smiled then said, "You are so perfect."

I don't know why I chose those words, they just came out before I could stop them.

She blushed then turned away, embarrassed about something. Why? I mean, the girl was pretty. She had been complimented before. I was sure of it.

An awkward silence fell over us. A silence that ate at my gut and needed to be ended now. "Where's Sara," I asked.

She pointed upstream. My sister sat on a large gray rock hugging her knees. Clancy lay at the bottom of the boulder, ready if she needed him. The horses had been staked out on a new piece of grass.

"What's wrong?" I asked.

Cassie spun and glared at me. "What's wrong? She lost her parents three months ago. Her brother almost died. Men were shooting at us, again! We're in the middle of nowhere. What's wrong?"

I sighed heavily then shook my head. My error. I shouldn't have asked. Grimacing I tried to get up.

"What are you doing?" Cassie snapped as she rushed back to hold me down.

"I'm going to go talk to my sister."

Cassie rolled her eyes. "She doesn't need you to fix anything."

I glared back as an anger began to build inside of me. "She's sad. Of course, she needs me to fix it."

Cassie glared at me for a moment then sighed and said. "She just wants to be alone for a few minutes. Give her time."

Girls. I swear I will never understand them. One minute she's being all caring, getting me painkillers, covering me in blankets. The next moment she's biting my head off for wanting to help my sister.

"Besides," Cassie continued as she draped another blanket over me. "You are on bed rest. We can't leave until you get better."

God I hate being fussed over but I could see this was a battle I wasn't going to win. So I settled with my back against the bluff and looked out over the distant country. Purple sage, and grassland. A sharp tangy dusty smell in the air with a hazy horizon.

How far? I wondered as I went over the mental map in my head. I was wrestling with boredom when Sara came back leading the horses. She gave me a quick smile then began helping Cassie.

Cassie shot me a glare with raised eyebrows as if saying, 'See, I told you so.'

All I could do was scoff to myself. I'd never figure them out. They were so different. Girls. But then, the image of Cassie in a wet T-shirt and tight jeans popped back into my head and I had to smile to myself. Thank God for those differences.

We headed out the next morning. Going North. I kept us on roads for a few miles to hide our trail then we cut across country. Wide open spaces without fences. We made Twenty-five miles each day for the next week. Climbing slowly as we worked our way up the foothills of the Rockies. Then finally moving into the mountains themselves.

We made a point of avoiding people. Towns, farms, anything. I got lucky and shot a large mule deer. We ate off him for almost eight days. In fact, the meat went bad before we could finish it all. Finally, we crossed over into what used to be Yellowstone Park.

"Why this way?" Cassie asked. "There has to be a dozen places we could have crossed over."

I shrugged then tried to hide my blush. "I always wanted to visit. I figure this is our last chance."

She shot me a confused look then laughed. "I guess it is as good a reason as any."

"Where are all the people," Sara asked. "The park gets thousands of people every day."

"The asteroid hit before the season started. We're pretty high up. It was still late winter in early April. None of the lodges and stuff were open yet."

Cassie shuddered. "Just think if all those people had been here. Twenty thousand people in cars that don't work. All stuck thousands of miles from home."

"Imagine Disney World, down in Florida," I said as a shiver ran down my back. "All those people trapped there. No food coming in. No working toilets. No way to get out except to walk. How many of them are from overseas? They'll never get home."

A sad quiet fell over us as we each thought about all the different scenarios where people could have been stuck. That could have been us. I knew Cassie was thinking about her family scattered across the country.

How many people were fighting to get home?

The park was mostly empty. Twice we saw people. One man on a horse in the distance but he kept away from us. Another couple walking south. They both waved but made a point of turning away from us.

People had become skittish, I realized. Probably with good reason.

But the park was so empty. This must have been what it was like when John Coulter found it. Of course, the Native Americans had been traveling through here for years. It was so easy to imagine Blackfeet or Crow Tee-Pees dotting the landscape.

We camped that night in a small bowl. I made sure to keep my rifle close and my Magnum .44 loose in its holster. This was bear country. And I was sleeping outside under the stars.

I made a point of working past the churning caldrons of steam and mud and one of the smaller guizers. We also saw a small herd of buffalo and another of elk slowly crossing the road.

Two days later we topped a ridge to find a campground full of people. Wow, I hadn't expected that. We'd been in the wilderness. Or at least what had felt like true wilderness.

I held up my hand to stop the girls while I studied the situation.

"Should we go around," Sara asked, pointing to a trail that skirted the campground.

Frowning, I studied them and shook my head. There must be a hundred people down there. Some in cars, some in tents. The grounds looked ... messy, was the best word. Stuff scattered and dropped on the ground. Too many people in one spot for too long.

"I want to talk to them," I said as I glanced over to make sure the girls were okay with it. We hadn't talked to anyone for so long. I wanted to know what had happened here. Who were these people and what were their plans?

A burning curiosity. I knew I might be making a mistake. But I just needed to know. Nudging Ajax I started down the hill. The girls fell in beside us. As we drew closer I shucked my rifle from its scabbard and rested it across my lap. But made a point of not pointing it at anyone. Just cool and calm.

A dozen people had moved to the edge of the campground watching us draw closer. I pulled up, making sure the girls stayed behind me then sat there and waited.

Finally, a mid-sized man with red hair and the beginning of a handlebar mustache stepped out and started towards us. He wore a Park Ranger's khaki shirt with a pistol on his hip.

As he drew closer I saw him study our horses and almost lick his lips. But he stopped himself then lifted a hand and smiled. "Hello, Name's Victor. You lot passing through or you looking for a place to settle?"

I leaned forward onto the saddle horn and nodded to the camp. Silently asking for an explanation.

He sighed heavily. "We heard about the asteroid a minute before everything went out. I got the report on my radio. Then nothing."

I nodded. "Yeah, airplanes falling from the sky. Cars not working. Phones out. An EMP."

He nodded then frowned. "We started with one hundred forty-nine people here in the campground. Another dozen setting up the lodge two miles down the road. A few on the road for day trips. The people at the lodge were mostly from out of state, here for the season, setting up. They hadn't gotten their food shipment in yet."

I cringed inside.

"Twenty of the campers decided to walk out." He paused for a moment then pointed to a new graveyard. "We lost another fourteen. Old folks mostly. They ran out of medicine. Heart attacks. One young girl with diabetes and no insulin. Three suicides."

Flinching, I could see it all and felt a sadness fill me. So much death. Every one a tragedy for someone's family.

"How are you feeding yourselves," Cassie asked as she walked her horse up next to mine.

The ranger smiled then said. "This is Yellowstone in the summer. The animals are so tame we can take one whenever we want. But that won't last. We're already seeing some of the herds getting skittish. By fall they'll be scattered into the backcountry. You just wait and see.

I thought about the animals we'd seen and had to chuckle to myself. We'd spent a hundred years not hunting them. Setting them up to be easy prey when the rules all changed.

"What about this winter?" I asked. "I heard it gets cold around here."

He laughed. "Colder than my ex-wife's heart. The b ... woman left me and moved to San Francisco. Said she wanted a life. Who marries a park ranger but wants to live in the city? Have you heard anything about the coast?"

I glanced over at Cassie who bit her lip. She didn't want to tell him that we suspected a tidal wave had wiped out half of California. Instead, I changed the subject, "So basically, you've established a new tribe for this area. The Blackfeet or Crow would be impressed."

He scoffed then nodded. "Yes, we're learning as we go. The Native Americans had generations of knowledge to pass down. We've got to learn it all over again. We'll move into the lodge for the winter. We can keep warm. We've got people gathering plants. We'll stock up on pine nuts. We're making Pemmican. We'll make it."

The determination in his eyes didn't waiver and I knew that they would. Or at least some of them would.

"Do you want to come in for dinner?" he asked. "We've got a fresh elk."

I glanced over at the girls and I could see their hesitation, We'd only made it this far because we avoided people. "Thanks anyway," I said as I looked up at the sun.

"We've still got an hour before we have to set up camp. We'll keep moving."

He frowned then said, "Any chance you want to part with one of those horses? You've got a spare. We'll trade."

I laughed. "There is nothing in this world you could give us more valuable than these horses."

He frowned then nodded. "I was afraid you'd say that. But I had to ask."

Smiling at him, I nodded with respect. Too many people would have tried to take our stuff. Especially the horses. This man wouldn't stoop down that low. He'd gone out of his way to care and organize this rag-tag bunch of strangers. Kept them focused and working to survive.

I honestly believe he was the type of man who could have lived off the land. All by himself. Deep in the woods. He would have made it easily. But he'd chosen to stay and help. My admiration for him grew. Would I have done the same?

Suddenly I felt a sense of guilt. Was I doing enough? What would Dad have wanted me to do? Should we stay and help? What could they accomplish with four horses?

But, as if seeing my hesitation, Sara stepped Brandy up even with us and said,

"We're headed to our people in Idaho. We wish you good luck."

The ranger frowned then let out a long breath and nodded. "Good luck to you three. I don't know which is worse. Being stuck here in the winter. Or up there?"

"They've got a farm," Cassie said. "It is easier to lay in enough food."

He nodded and I could see his mind working. It was too late to start this year. Next year they would have time to plant. God, I hoped they made it that far.

Tipping my hat to him, I pulled Ajax to the side and started to work around the campground. No, I wasn't going to stay and help. My responsibility was to the girls. My mission. Our quest, get to Cassie's family.

Basically, nothing else mattered. It had to be that way. I had to maintain a narrow focus or we'd never succeed.

Chapter Twenty

Cassie

My heart ached when I looked over my shoulder at those people in the campground. There had been so many children. Would they make it? Would any of us? Or was humanity on the way out?

Glancing over at Luke and Sara I felt my heart fill back up with love. I was so lucky to have them. Two friends who had sacrificed so much. People I could rely on. People I could trust. Yes, I might very well be one of the luckiest girls within a thousand miles.

The world as I knew it was gone. My family dispersed across the continent. My mother had died. Mr. and Mrs. Thompson had died. So many people had died. But I was alive, with friends I could trust. Enroute to my family. Yes, I was the lucky one.

Of course, as soon as I thought about my good fortune. I realized it could all disappear so fast. That was my new world. The realization that there was no safety. No place I could go and feel secure.

We rode for another hour when Luke pointed out a steaming pool that spilled over into a trickle down to a creek. A hot spring. "A bath?" he said with a smile. "I bet the creek water is warm enough without being too hot."

My heart jumped at the thought of being clean. We'd been on the road for so long. We'd run out of baby wipes weeks ago. It had been washcloths and cold water ever since.

We set up camp in the trees next to the creek. Once we were done Luke reached behind his back and pulled off his shirt. "I'm first."

I froze and stared at those wide shoulders narrowing down to slim hips.

He gingerly removed the bandage on his side. The wound had closed up. He folded his shirt then laughed as he dropped his gun belt and began to remove his pants. Suddenly he froze when he caught me staring at him.

His cheeks flashed red. "I'll be right back," he said as he wove through the trees down to the creek.

I glanced over at Sara, she was staring at me with a strange expression. I fought to hide the emotions racing through me. The boy was just so delectable. Of course I was going to stare at him. What girl wouldn't?

Suddenly the horses started stomping shifting back and forth upset. I turned just as a whiff of pig hit me. That pork stink of a pigsty. Confused, I was about to ask Sara if she smelled it when a yell from the creek made my soul freeze. Luke!

Without thinking, I grabbed my rifle and was about to race to him when he dashed through the trees in nothing but his shorts. A rather large and fearsome grizzly chasing him. It was only the thick brush and trees that slowed the bear down enough for me to lift my rifle and fire.

The rifle fired. Nothing. I knew I hit him, he was so big he was impossible to miss. But he shook it off and continued chasing Luke.

I jacked another round into the chamber and fired just as Luke raced past me. Again nothing. Had I missed?

The bear suddenly slammed to a stop and raised up as Clancy barked and nipped at him. Twisting he swung at Clancy as the dog danced out of the way.

My heart pounded as all noise disappeared from the world. There was just the bear. Just my death.

I fired for the third time and saw my shot hit him high on the right shoulder. Again, nothing. He didn't fall, didn't react. Instead, he twisted and stared at me with cold, soulless eyes that turned my stomach to water. Pure death and I was his focus.

Freezing, I waited to die when an explosion to my side made me jump and forced me out of my stupor. The bear lifted up and growled as another explosion erupted next to me then the bear fell. Half of his head missing.

Luke stood there, his magnum .44 leaking smoke, still pointed at the bear. Standing in nothing but his shorts. As steady as a rock, the gun never wavering. The look in his eyes reminded me of the bear's. A deadly stare that ensured death to any that threatened him or his.

My heart melted for the thousandth time. Once more he'd saved me. How many times can a boy save a girl's life and she not yell to the world that she loved him?

Finally, I saw his muscles relax as he took a deep breath. "He came out of nowhere."

I nodded.

Sara joined us. "I was trying to get my shotgun. By the time I had it ready you already killed him."

The three of us stood there and looked at the dead bear in the middle of our camp. It was strange, one moment we were all focused on the bear, and the next I was very aware of how close to naked Luke was and had to fight to keep my eyes from drifting over to examine him.

No one said anything but the tension was there.

He cussed under his breath. "I'll go get my clothes. Saddle Ajax for me. I'll go tell those campers they can have a thousand pounds of grizzly meat if they want it. I don't want to spend the next two days harvesting him."

"I'll go," Sara said as she started for Brandy. "You need to rest."

"I need a bath," he cursed.

Without thinking I said, "I'll stand guard."

Sara shot me a look then shook her head as she saddled her horse. Was I being too obvious? No, no way did she know how I felt about her brother. She would have yelled at me and hated me forever.

Ten minutes later she gave us a quick wave and was off. Luke glanced over at me then started back down to the creek only this time he carried both his pistol and his rifle and a fresh set of clean clothes. The last set he owned.

The creek bubbled along. A pool had been formed behind some rocks, a good three feet deep with a sandy bottom. It looked so enticing.

"It's warm," Luke said as he dipped a toe in then gave me a strange look before stepping into the pool and dipping down, coming up spitting water and smiling like a little kid at Christmas.

He shook his head and said, "You're supposed to be standing guard, not watching me."

I gulped as I fought to stop blushing then turned my back and focused on the distant countryside. All the while I could hear Luke behind me washing, first himself then his clothes. A dozen images danced through my mind.

Finally, I heard him step out and froze, too afraid to turn around.

"Okay," he said. "Your turn."

I turned to find him wrapped in a towel, bent over, laying his wet clothes on the rocks to dry.

"I didn't bring my clothes," I said as I turned to hurry back to camp. I needed distance. Sometimes it was just too much being around Luke Thompson.

When I got back down to the creek He was already dressed and using his fingers to rake his wet hair out of his eyes. I froze and admired the man until he caught me staring. "Like I said, your turn."

He belted on his pistol then grabbed his rifle and turned to face the distant horizon. Clancy took up position on this side of the creek, keeping an eye on the trees.

I froze, Luke expected me to undress and take a bath with him only a dozen feet away. As if reading my mind, he glanced over his shoulder and said, "You need to hurry, Sara is going to be back with those campers and you don't want them finding you naked and neck deep in a creek."

I swallowed hard and nodded. He turned back away. My fingers shook and my heart raced but I eventually got into the creek. He was right. It was warm. Not too hot. I'm sure if we moved fifty feet up to the steaming spring it'd burn our skin, but this was perfect, and unlike the baths at home, the water never cooled down.

As I washed, I made sure to focus on Luke's back, terrified he'd turn around. Why? I wondered. Any other person I would have been mad. But for some reason, Luke seeing me like this made my insides quiver with pure fear.

Why? Because he might not like what he saw, I realized. I mean, this was Luke Thompson. The boy could have almost any girl in school. I would be competing against a long line of pretty girls.

Sighing, I pushed the thought away and focused on getting clean. I had to use the bar soap to wash my hair, twice. But finally, I felt clean for the first time in weeks. Sighing I said, "I'm getting out."

He started to turn but stopped and nodded.

I hesitated then hurried out into a towel and spent a few minutes drying my hair.

Luke gave the area one more scan then turned back and froze, his eyes traveling up over my towel-clad body with a hungry look that made me freeze.

The two of us stood there staring at each other when Clancy barked, breaking the tension between us.

Sara had returned with a dozen men from the campground. Victor broke away and walked down to us. He stared at me standing there in nothing but a towel then pointed back up at the dead bear.

"Thanks."

Luke nodded then said, "Thank Cassie, if she hadn't shot it I never would have had time to get to my gun."

Victor nodded and smiled at me then turned to go back and help his men prepare the bear.

We stayed out of their way and it didn't take them more than an hour to have that bear skinned, carved up, and the meat divided amongst the men and headed back to their camp just as the sun dipped down below the western horizon.

After the last man had left with the rolled-up skin on his shoulder, Victor held out his hand for Luke. "You don't know how much this is going to help. Especially the bear fat. The kids, they're not getting enough fat in their diets. None of us are. But the kids need it. We'll use it in the pemmican."

Luke nodded then shrugged, that eternal cool attitude. No big deal, he killed grizzlies and saved strangers every day.

As I lay in our tent that night a thought danced through my mind, the memory of that look in his eyes when he saw me in the towel. Combine that with him calling my name in his sleep. Suddenly my heart fluttered. Was it possible?

Then Sara snorted in her sleep as she turned over and the reality hit me. Even if by some miracle Luke was interested in me. He would never do anything about it. Sara would hate him and he'd never hurt her. One of the many things I loved about him.

Sighing, I pushed the unhappiness out of my heart. Life sucked in so many ways. But then I smiled as I remembered that hungry look in his eyes. At least I had that.

Chapter Twenty-One

Luke

I spent that night with my pistol in hand curled under the saddle I used as my pillow. I'd been such a fool. Going down to the creek without my gun. A stupider move was impossible. But in my defense, I'd caught that look in Cassie's eyes and my mind had wandered to thoughts it shouldn't.

I know. Stupid. My dad would have been furious at me. A man couldn't afford to make those kinds of mistakes. My job. My only job was to get the girls to safety. If I was so stupid about a simple thing like going armed in bear country. What else was I screwing up?

The morning found me curled up, shivering. I cracked one eye to see the gray morning sky with just enough light to find a strange white dusting everywhere.

"What the ... ?" I muttered as I sat up, keeping the blanket tight. Snow! In July? "Hey," I yelled for the girls. This wasn't right. Even this high. We were over a mile up. But snow in July?

"Hey," I yelled again. I needed the girls to see this just to make sure I wasn't hallucinating. Had that run-in with the bear screwed up my brain or something?

Cassie stuck her head out the tent zipper. My heart jumped. She was gorgeous with mussed-up hair and sleepy eyes. Suddenly, her eyes widened in surprise. Good, she saw it too.

"Snow?" she gasped.

I shivered as I looked around. A light dusting. It'd be burnt off by noon. Shaking my head, I grabbed my jacket from my saddle then shook out my boots before slamming my feet into them. "We need to get going," I told her just as Sara stuck her head out above Cassie. "We don't know if this is the beginning or the end.

Cassie frowned then scurried out, "It's July," Cassie said, "July twelfth I think."

Sara gasped, "Oh Cassie, it was your birthday six days ago. I'm sorry."

Cassie smiled at her friend and then shrugged. "Birthdays don't matter. And if I romember. We were worried about Luke getting shot. My birthday didn't seem that important."

Sighing heavily, Sara scrambled out but I knew my sister. She'd beat herself up for two days about forgetting her best friend's birthday. But how could you blame her? We didn't keep track of days. I was sort of amazed that Cassie did. But then that was like her. Always surprising me.

We grabbed a quick breakfast then hit the trail. We worked our way out of the park and into Montanna, down a long valley. The mountain tops were all capped in snowy white. Cassie caught me staring and said, "The asteroid. The haze. It threw up so much dust it blocked the sun. Cooling things down. All summer, I've noticed this has to be the coolest summer ever. It's barely gotten over eighty in the hottest parts of the country."

I nodded as I examined the sky. There was the permanent haze. Not obvious. But there.

"I thought the asteroid hit in the ocean," Sara said.

Cassie nodded. "The oceans are about a thousand feet deep maybe two. That's a third of a mile deep. They were saying the asteroid was I think about two and a half miles long. It buried itself in the ocean floor."

Sara nodded. I smiled to myself. There is something about a smart girl which was just naturally sexy as hell. Especially when she was wearing tight jeans, sitting on the back of a horse, her hair in a ponytail.

God, I had it bad I realized. This was my sister's best friend, I reminded myself for the thousandth time. Then it hit me. Birthday. She was now seventeen. For some reason that made things worse. Or better, depending on how you looked at it.

We took two days to hit I-90 just west of Bozeman Montana. As always, we avoided people wherever possible. The country was mostly farms. Unfortunately, it looked like a lot of it was alfalfa.

It didn't matter I realized. Nothing had been planted. And if it had they didn't have working irrigation to water the crops. The pumps wouldn't work. Cringing, I shook my head. Places like this would do better than others. But it wasn't going to be enough. I just knew it.

After we hit I-90 I kept us on the highway for a while. That snow back there was like a kick in the pants. We needed to get to Idaho. The highway was the shortest, easiest route. Although littered with abandoned cars, there were few people.

Where had they all gone? Towns? Had the farmers taken them in? Or ... a sick feeling filled me. How many had died trying to get home?

We passed farmhouses but no tractors out in the field. Nobody putting in crops to be harvested this fall. My gut tightened. Things were going to go from bad to worse to terrible. This winter was going to kill millions. Tens of millions.

But it was the cities that were the worst. The small towns not so much. They were close to the farms. Grain silos, pigs, chickens. Food was traded.

The cities like Bozeman were hurting. I shuddered thinking about the big cities, what was Denver like. New York, Chicago? How much food did they have? Two weeks? It had been a little over three months since the asteroid hit. No trucks, no trains, nothing to deliver food to the cities.

So we avoided the cities, going out of our way. I sat on Ajax and ran through some calculations, reviewing our trip. I bet we had added two weeks of travel time working our way around cities and towns.

We worked our way through the mountains, up one ridge, down another valley, wash and repeat.

Cimarron picked up a stone, I cleaned it out but he needed a day of rest. Cassie rode behind Sara so we could keep making progress.

My mind flashed back to that time she'd ridden behind me. Again. I fought to keep my thoughts where they belonged.

Two days later we were back to normal when we were approaching the small town of Missoula. I wanted to avoid towns but it was impossible to get past without heading up into the forest on some firebreak trail and

I didn't know this country. We'd get lost and spend an extra month working our way out.

Instead, we were forced to approach the town.

A dozen barriers had been placed across the highway. Both sides and the grassy median between them.

Two cops stood behind a car, one held up his hand.

I swallowed hard and got down, handed my reins to Cassie then approached. "We just want to get to Idaho."

The taller one laughed, "They ain't letting people in. Smart if you ask me. You people think you can just show up and take what doesn't belong to you."

I felt my brow furrow in confusion Where was this coming from?

Examining them I felt my stomach tighten. They both looked skinny. Not natural skinny. And their uniforms hung on them like they'd both dropped a lot of weight recently. A hungry man could be dangerous I thought.

"We just want to get through. We won't stop."

His eyes narrowed as he studied me, then the girls on the horses. I could read his mind. Horses could feed a lot of people.

"Okay," he said then nodded to his partner who turned and hurried towards the town., "Let me get my people. They'll escort you through."

My stomach tightened down even more as a series of bells and whistles started going off in my head. I could see it in his eyes. That feral look of a predator who had his prey in sight. Nothing would stop him. To fail was to die of starvation.

When his people showed up they were going to take our horses. And if they had to kill us, no big deal. Less mouths to feed.

Swallowing hard, I nodded then said, "Okay, I'll go get the others." As I turned I expected a bullet to the back. I think it was only the fact that the girls were so far back and he wanted all four horses.

Both Cassie and Sara started walking the horses towards me. A sudden fear of them getting into range shot through me. That cop would kill us in an instant. Our horses would feed his family for the winter. Our death might mean his children surviving.

It really had come down to this.

When I got to them I let out a long breath and swung up onto Ajax. Both girls raised their eyebrows silently asking me what was going on.

"I think we need to go around," I told them. "Something isn't right."

Both girls immediately looked at the cop then back at me.

The cop waived his arm for us to hurry. Like if we didn't they might change their minds.

I examined the road into town. Twenty thousand people. I then looked up at the forest-covered mountains surrounding the town.

"It's up to you," Cassie said and gave me an encouraging smile. Sara nodded in agreement.

I sighed then turned Ajax to head back down the road.

"Hey," the cop yelled as he came out from behind his cruiser.

Clicking my tongue I worked Ajax up into a lope and got us away from that cop before he and his friends tried to take what they needed.

It took me an hour to find a firebreak and work our way up into the mountains. Another two days to get around the town using a combination of fire roads and game trails.

Only when we were on the other side, five miles past the town was I able to relax. Two and a half days added to the trip. It pissed me off, but deep in my gut I knew we'd done the right thing.

It took us another ten days to make the Idaho border. Each morning I would wake up with a dread in the pit of my stomach. Would today be the day we failed? The day this new cruel world killed us.

And what had that cop meant by not letting people in? They couldn't keep people out of a state. Could they?

Each night, around the campfire, we'd stare into the flames, each lost in our own thoughts. What we had lost. What we would face. Our past and our future.

"The rules have changed," Cassie suddenly blurted out one night as she tossed a twig onto the fire.

"No duh," Sara said mockingly.

Cassie looked up and stared at me as if trying to send me a message. "No, the rules have changed. All of them. Social expectations. Relationships. Everything is different."

My gut dropped. Was she trying to tell me something? There was a look in her eyes as if she was begging me to understand.

I noticed Sara glancing at her then at me. Her frown told me exactly what she was thinking. Then it hit me. Did Sara think Cassie liked me? No way?

But my gut told me differently. That look in Cassie's eyes told me so much. My world shifted on itself What was she saying? No this was impossible. I couldn't hurt Sara like that. She'd been hurt enough.

Staring down into the fire I let the tension melt away. Cassie sighed heavily then said good night before getting up and going to the tent.

Sara glared at me as if I'd done something terrible. What? I was screwed either way. I hurt Cassie or I hurt Sara. And both of them meant too much to me to ever be hurt. Especially by me.

Luckily. The next morning, Cassie acted like nothing happened which made me think it hadn't. I'd imagined that look in the dark. Her words had been misunderstood. I was an idiot who didn't know better.

As we drew closer to the Idaho border I began to fight a nervousness deep inside of my gut. Something bad was going to happen, I just knew it.

A barrier three feet high and a foot thick of logs had been placed across the road. Barbed wire fences reached out from the barrier. Trees had been cleared marking the border.

Four soldiers manned the barrier, machine guns slung over their shoulders, staring at us like we were vermin infesting their homes.

"Names?" the Corporal said as he stared at me. His glare dropped to the pistol on my hip then the rifles in our scabbards. The man was cataloging threats and dangers. Cool, I couldn't blame him.

"We're going to my grandfather's farm," Cassie said as if that gave her all the authority she would ever need.

The soldier scoffed then shook his head, "Everyone and their uncle has a grandfather up in the mountains. Believe me. I've heard it all. Names."

I let out a long breath to try and calm my racing heart. I hate being told what to do. Especially by egotistical power-hungry idiots like this guy. Only when I had myself back under control did I give him our names.

He flipped through some pages on a clipboard then frowned and looked up. "If you're lying ..."

"Why would we lie?" Cassie asked.

He continued to stare down the list then sighed heavily. "How about Jim and Milly Thompson? They're on the list also. Where are they?"

Sara gasped.

"They're dead," I said as I stared down at him. "The first day. A jet airplane landed on their heads."

The soldier had the good grace to wince then nodded.

Cassie inched forward. "What would have happened if we weren't on the list?"

Shrugging, he said, "You'd have been shot for trying to cross. We don't even yell a warning anymore. Just shoot on sight."

My gut tightened when I realized he wasn't lying.

Cassie frowned, "How did we get on the list? We're from Oklahoma. Who put us on the list?"

The soldier turned and pointed to another soldier walking down the trail toward the barrier. "Him," he said as if that explained everything.

Cassie looked up and gasped. "Tim? Time Devo?"

Chapter Twenty-Two

Cassie

I couldn't believe it. A part of my past. From before. A small part of my family's story. Tim Devo.

"Cassie Conrad," he said shaking his head as he drew closer. "Finally. A complete set."

My brow furrowed as I tried to work out what he was talking about. I was still in a foggy confusion. How was this possible? He was dressed like a soldier. With two stripes on his upper arm.

"Tim?" I gasped. I know, I am quick on the uptake.

He smiled then glanced at first Luke then over at Sara. Suddenly his eyes widened and he smiled. That smile boys get when they see something they like.

Sara blushed deep red.

Tim pulled his eyes away from her, reluctantly I would have said, and nodded to Luke. He could tell who was in charge. "Ryan, Cassie's brother asked me to put you all on the list.

Again he glanced over at Sara, "One of my better moves."

"Ryan?" I gasped. "You saw my brother. Is he okay?"

Tim nodded, glancing over at Sara again before saying, "Got a letter from him a month ago, via my Mom. He gave me your guy's names and asked I add you to the lists. That list has become sort of famous. It is literally life or death sometimes." Then he turned to me and said, "They're all doing fine."

"They?" I asked as I held my breath. "Haley? Chase?"

He smiled then nodded back over his shoulder. "Come on. You can set up camp on the base. We've got food. It's free the first night. After that visitors are on their own. Unless you move into one of the camps." Again he glanced at Sara. Okay, the boy was way interested.

They were alive. They had made it to Papa's farm. How? My heart soared. "Chase and Haley," I demanded.

"Yes, yes," he said. "They're fine. You should see Haley's new boyfriend, he's the size of a small mountain and just as hard. And Ryan's girlfriend is just as sweet as Chase's girlfriend."

What did Papa think of these new people? Knowing him he'd be sweet to the girlfriends and tough with Haley's boyfriend. Suddenly I thought of my father and Luke.

What would he think if he knew about how I felt about Luke. I almost laughed out loud. It didn't matter how I felt. Nothing was ever going to happen.

My stomach cinched up tight. My family was changing. My brother had a girlfriend and I hadn't met her. How was that possible? It also seemed like everyone had paired up. Suddenly my insides hardened into a rock as I realized I would be the only one alone.

Especially if Sara gave Tim even the slightest hint that she was interested. Which she totally was.

"Come on," Tim said as he told the other soldiers to pull the fence back and let us in.

Fifteen minutes later he pointed out where we could make our camp and the food tent. "I've got to go tell the Captain about you lot. He'll want to hear your story. We've also got a blacksmith slash farrier. We'll get the horses shod and some oats."

"What do you want in exchange?" Luke asked with a scowl.

Tim laughed. "Help moving some horses north. You'll see."

I watched him walk away as my mind tumbled over itself as a sense of relief filled me. We were in. My family was safe. How had we met Tim here in the middle of nowhere?

"Who is that?" Sara hissed at me.

"Tim Devo," I told her. "He was a friend of Ryan's and Chase's. He lived about a mile from my Papa's farm. We'd hang out every summer when we came to visit."

She looked after him then quietly glanced over at her brother before helping me finish setting up the tent. When we started getting firewood she hissed. "What do you know about him?"

I frowned at her and almost asked who, just to tease her but I knew what she wanted. And I'm not that mean. Not most of the time. "My brother's friend. Not much to know. We'd visit in the summer. They'd go hunting and camping together. He had a crush on Haley..."

"Your cousin?"

"Yeah, but it sounds like she's got a boyfriend now."

Sara looked up the trail to where Tim had gone then sighed heavily.

I almost laughed. She'd barely met the boy and now she was interested all because he stared at her.

"Why is he in the Army?"

Shrugging, I said, "I don't know. You'll have to ask him."

Luke finished taking care of the horses when Tim returned with an officer. He made the introductions. Luke informed this Captain Mullan all about our trip. What we'd seen, our route, what things were like down in Oklahoma. I did notice he didn't say anything about being shot or killing those men.

Finally, the Captain nodded and welcomed us to Idaho. "You're lucky. If you're people hadn't gotten you on that list you wouldn't be let in. I'll want you to write up a report tonight so I can forward it tomorrow. Just a couple of pages laying out what you just told me."

I glanced over at Tim but he was staring at Sara like a lost puppy. She was blushing and making a point of not looking at him.

"Come on," he said, "I'll show you where to get food."

We followed him into a large green tent the size of a basketball court. As we stood in line he kept glancing over his shoulder at Sara. I swear it was getting annoying. "So," I said, pulling his attention away from her. "Why are you in the Army?"

He laughed then said, "Junior ROTC. In high school. It was my route to college, a foot in the door for regular ROTC. A few years in the National Guard and I leave with an engineering degree. That was the plan. When the rock hit, They activated all of us into the guard."

"Are they taking new people?" Luke asked.

My stomach tightened. No way was he thinking about joining the army. Please no.

Tim shrugged. "The call-up was for six months. I've only got two more to go. But yeah, they are always looking for new people. Hell, you know they're short-handed. They made me a corporal."

Sara asked, "Are you going to reenlist?"

Tim smiled then said, "I was thinking about maybe doing that. I get fed, and the job is cool. But I don't know. Winter is coming on and my folks are all alone." He paused then smiled again, "Besides, That part of Idaho is going to be very interesting real soon "

She blushed again and looked away, but I saw the secret smile in her eyes.

We sat down at a long table. There were about a dozen men and women in uniform scattered in small groups. I noticed that Luke maneuvered to sit next to Tim as he shot his sister a concerned look. I had to look down to hide my smile. Luke was worried about his sister. For good reason. I knew her. She didn't blush easily. And she couldn't seem to stop around this guy.

We ate our stew as Tim informed us about what had happened. Haley's boyfriend going to prison camp and escaping. Chase helping get food wagons through. Ryan sneaking into Idaho with a handful of refugees.

"We're starting to get back on our feet," he said. "No electricity except what can be created locally. Solar doesn't work. The stuff was all burnt out by the EMP. All the regular transformers are fried and we're never going to get new ones. Electrical switches, generators. Everything is gone. Vehicles are dead so horses are king again. It looks like you've got some good ones. The Army will buy them if you want."

"What are the roads like?" Luke asked ignoring the suggestion to sell the horses. "I mean danger-wise?"

Tim shrugged. "We're hearing reports. Some areas are worse than others. They leave the army alone. But ..."

Luke nodded. Things hadn't changed we would be responsible for our own safety.

"What about food?" I asked.

Tim smiled. "We think we're going to have enough to get people through the winter. But the problem is getting it to them. Especially after the snows set in. You had

246

better be set up by then or you're not going to make it until spring. And that is all from last year's crop. Next year is going to be so much worse."

A cold shiver ran down my back as I imagined how many people would starve to death this winter.

It was strange though. We seemed to put aside the fear and worry. We had changed I realized. As a people. There was no time to sit and worry. You either did things to help survive. Or you died.

We sat and talked. Laughing as Tim told stories about Ryan and Chase. I brought up how Chase had scared him off when he found out Tim had a crush on Haley.

"Hey, I was thirteen," Tim moaned. Then glanced over at Sara to see if she was upset.

Luke glared at him and said, "Hey, that is what brothers are for."

Tim nodded then looked at me then at him. "Yeah, well, when you get there. Ryan isn't going to be happy about you and Cassie. I promise you."

"What?" I gasped. "No. Um. No. You're wrong. It's not like that." My insides squeezed shut with pure embarrassment.

Tim frowned looking back and forth between us then over at Sara.

"You are wrong," Luke said. "There is nothing between Cassie and me. She's just my sister's friend."

Tim frowned then shrugged. "Okay, If you say so. But the way you two look at each other. I mean, you see it don't you Sara."

My best friend stared at me with a furrowed brown then said. "So this crush on Haley. I remember her. She was very cute."

Tim rolled his eyes. It was obvious Sara had changed the subject but she was a pretty girl so he wasn't going to push her on it. Instead, he shrugged. "Yeah. But like I said, her boyfriend is the size of Montana. And she is very much in love. And hey, I was thirteen. I'd have crushed on any girl who was willing to talk to me."

Again he glanced at me and I could see it in his eyes. His belief that I was in love with Luke.

A heavy tension fell over us and rested above the group for the rest of the evening. I made a point of going to bed early that night. I didn't want to see the questioning look in Sara's eyes nor see Luke shudder at the idea of being pared with me. That would be a hurt-too-much type moment. After all, I was only Sara's friend.

The next morning over breakfast I was debating with myself whether to address the issue with Luke when someone yelled, "POOOOONNNNEEYYY."

Both Sara and I turned to see a horseman bent forward, racing into camp. The horse was covered in a foamy lather, breathing hard. The chestnut slammed to a halt in front of a corral.

A girl, in uniform, jumped from the horse. She was about my age. She tossed a packet of letters to another soldier as he gave her a packet of letters in return. She stuffed them into a saddlebag before jumping on the back of a new horse. She'd barely gotten her boots into the stirrups when she spurred the horse and they were off.

The three of us stood there, our jaws open, the girl had come and gone in a minute.

Tim approached, smiling from ear to ear. "Pony Express."

"Wow," Luke said with admiration.

"A girl?" Sara said.

Tim nodded. "Most of us did it at the beginning. Riding dispatch. But we found that girls were just lighter, could go faster, farther. Besides, most of them grew up riding horses. And like I said. No one messes with the army or we cut off food to their region. The people would lynch them in an instant for threatening that.

"We set up stations every ten miles with new horses. I just sent a letter to my mom. I got a buddy up north who will get it to her. I get his letters to his sister over in Peacock. She'll get word to your people."

My heart jumped at the thought of them knowing I was all right.

"How long?" I asked.

"Two days," he said. "A rider will put in about a hundred miles. Ten stops, in eight hours. In fact, I'm taking some horses to the stations up the trail. Thought we might go together. The Captain's okayed it. One less person he has to send. And like I said, it gets your horses new shoes and fresh oats." Again he glanced over at Sara. I swear the boy was so obvious, and Sara was loving it.

Luke nodded but then frowned when he saw his sister smile at Tim. I had to fight to not laugh. Both of them were so obvious. Suddenly a pang of jealousy shot through me. It wasn't fair. Sara could flirt and smile. Luke couldn't stop her. She wasn't breaking a taboo about a girl's best friend never falling for her brother.

No, it just wasn't fair.

Chapter Twenty-Three

Luke

I didn't know what to think about this Tim guy. He seemed okay. And yes, I was very aware that he was interested in my sister. Every nerve in my body was telling me to scare him off. But I knew Sara, she'd clean my clock if I tried that. I'd wake up to burnt breakfasts for a weak and rocks under my sleeping bag all the way there.

Besides, we were separating from him in a couple of days so no big deal. They wouldn't be alone. I know, old fashioned. But things had changed. There was a reason the males of a family were concerned about their female relatives. Even more so in this new world.

And hey, I am not a complete troglodyte. I didn't mind my sister having a boyfriend. As long as he was a good guy. But like I said, we were separating so this guy wasn't boyfriend material. He might be a good guy, but if he wasn't I'd end him in a quick minute.

We left the next morning. Tim had been good to his word. All new shoes for the horses and forty pounds of oats. He'd even gotten us ten pounds of dog food for Clancy. I noticed that he made a point of giving it to Sara. Like he was the great savior.

She'd blushed. Again something new. My sister wasn't the blushing type. Who was this guy and how did he have her all twisted up in knots?

He was leading six horses strung together on a long lead. We were maybe a mile out of camp when Sara nudged Brandy forward so she could ride next to him. I turned to Cassie. She laughed and shook her head.

"He is a nice guy. I promise."

I harrumphed. But as we rode I noticed that Sara would lean towards him when she talked. As if she was worried I might hear her.

But as the day grew hot I began to relax. Like I had said, we were separating in a couple of days.

We stopped for lunch next to a creek and a patch of grass. The countryside was rolling hills, grassland broken up by pine trees and quick streams. Behind the hills were more mountains with white caps even in July.

Tim caught me staring at the mountains and said, "Yeah, the snow hasn't melted this year. It's going to be a bitch of a winter."

"What do you hear, about the rest of the country."

He shook his head. "We get reports. People like you coming from all over. People on the list. Some places are better than others. Places with farms. Silos full of grain. Other places..." Here he shuddered. "Cities burning, civil war in some places. Gangs forming, taking what they need. It isn't pretty."

I nodded. "Yeah, we saw some of that on the way up here."

"Believe me, it is way worse back east. Like I said, we might have enough food in stock to feed the whole state. At least this year. But there's no way to get it to them. We've set up camps. And we're distributing to some of the cities. But it's not going to be enough."

"I'm surprised there isn't mass migration. From the other states. People leaving the cities. I mean, you might be the army. But a couple thousand people could swarm you guys no problem. Let alone a million."

Tim scoffed as he nodded. "Believe me, I know. We used to talk about it. Us enlisted guys, in our tents at night. If they ordered us to, could we open fire to stop people? Families? Kids? If we didn't, would our families die? Would we be court-martialed and hung the next morning?"

"What did you decide?" Sara asked.

He paused for a long moment then said, "We never really decided one way or the other. We all just prayed it didn't happen."

"And it hasn't," I said. "Not yet."

Tim nodded. "Give it time. I'll be honest. I'm hoping I'm out of the Army before they show up. If they get all the way to Elmira Idaho, then it's already too late."

We sat there in somber silence, each thinking about a mob of people storming our homes looking for food."

"What about the coasts," Cassie asked. "Dad was ten miles from the beach."

Tim's brow furrowed as he stared down. "Ryan told me the wave was a mile high. It washed up against the mountains fifteen miles inland."

Cassie cringed. I quickly said, "But you said he got away."

"Yes, he did. Barely."

I turned to Cassie, "Your dad's a smart man. He will know what to do."

She smiled sadly at me, silently thanking me.

Again an awkward silence fell over us until it was time to start again. We stopped at the next station to leave two horses behind then continued on, setting up camp next to a stream. Tim had been right. People didn't bother the Army. His uniform was like a get-out-of-jail-free card. They smiled. Little children waved. Their parents asked if we needed anything. It was so different.

The people in charge of food distribution had become the most important people in the world.

Sara kept looking at Tim with a strange expression. As if she was reevaluating things.

We hit the creek and had half a dozen trout in ten minutes. Sara took them from me. It was my turn to cook dinner but she insisted. Cassie couldn't stop a smile then nodded for me to follow her.

It was still a couple hours from sundown. Sunset is late in the north at that time of summer. We walked off a little way along the creek when she touched my shoulder and said, "She wants to impress Tim."

"I know," I cursed as I threw a stick for Chancy to fetch. He rushed off into the brush and returned with the exact stick I'd thrown.

"Luke," she admonished. "She has smiled more in the last two days than the previous three months. Don't you dare ruin this for her."

I growled under my breath.

"For the first time," she continued. "She's looking towards the future, not the past."

Sighing, I nodded. "We're separating tomorrow."

Cassie rolled her eyes as she started to climb the boulders next to the creek. We were out of sight of camp. I didn't know if Cassie had pulled me away to give her friend alone time with Tim. Or if there was something else.

She pushed up to the second layer of boulders. I was about to tell her to be careful when a quick rattle made my world slam to a halt. That sickening sound every western child learns to fear. Cassie's face went white as she squealed and fell back.

I don't know how, But I was there to catch her. She fell into my arms like she was designed to fit.

Freezing, I stared down into her eyes. "Are you all right? Did you get bit?"

She swallowed hard then shook her head. "No. He warned me and I twisted to get away and fell."

Letting out a long breath I continued to stare at her, unwilling to set her down. She stared back up at me. Her eyes searched mine as she licked her lips. A strange expression on her face.

My heart raced, without thinking things through. Without stopping myself, I leaned down and kissed her. Not a quick peck, but an adult kiss.

She seemed to sink into me as she wrapped her hands around my neck and held me tighter as the kiss became hot and heavy. I became lost until I heard Sara calling my name.

"Luke? Cassie?"

I pulled back, staring down at Cassie, silently asking her what she thought.

She frowned then said, "You better put me down."

Nodding, I reluctantly put her down on her feet just before Sara came around the bend in the trial.

Biting my lip I tried to not look guilty but I couldn't help but notice Cassie's ponytail had come undone. And her lips looked swollen. Had we really kissed that hard?

"Tim's said there is a town about a mile east of here. We can see some smoke from chimneys. He's going in to get a report. His captain wants to know some things. He said he'll be back before dark."

She suddenly frowned, her brow narrowing as she looked at Cassie, then back at me.

My gut tightened. I didn't want to have this fight. Not then. I was still trying to figure stuff out. I swallowed as I gently pulled Cassie away from the boulder. "You two stay back, there is a rattlesnake up in those rocks."

Sara's frown deepened before she shrugged then turned to head back to camp. I glanced over at Cassie but she wouldn't look at me. Great. I had ruined everything. She was going to hate me. When Sara got far enough in front I leaned down and whispered, "I'm sorry."

She slammed to a halt then hissed, "Don't you dare act like it was nothing."

The anger in her eyes put a hitch in my heartbeat. Had I really screwed up? "It won't ..."

"No," she gasped as she grabbed my arm. "Don't you dare act like it was not important? That was the greatest kiss in the history of kisses and I will not have you dismiss it as unimportant. I am not too young. You aren't the first boy to kiss me. Believe me. I know what that meant."

I froze, confused. Why was she acting like this?

She looked down the trail to Sara then back up at me and shook her head, "And don't tell me that you would never do anything to hurt Sara. That Sara is my best friend. Believe me, I know."

And with that, she stormed off leaving me to stare after her confused out of my gourd. Girls?

But then I remembered that kiss and smiled to myself. Sure, my life was screwed a thousand different ways but I couldn't forget the way she felt in my arms. The taste of her lips and the way my world felt holding her. Better. As if everything made sense.

That night, I lay under the stars staring up at them as I tried to figure out what I was going to do. First off, my sister would kill me if she found out I was kissing her best friend. But another part of me wanted to tell her to grow up and get over it.

I mean, who could blame me? Cassie was beautiful, smart, sweet, calm, and have I said beautiful. I mean heart-stopping gorgeous. Girl next door perfect kind of pretty. Okay, I realized I was breaking a dozen rules. But tough.

The next morning Tim caught me staring at Cassie as she bent over the pot of oatmeal on the fire. I quickly looked away but not before he gave me a knowing look then just smiled.

I ground my teeth. What was I going to do? Deny it? He hadn't said anything. And the more I protested the dumber I would sound.

A couple of hours, I told myself then we'd be rid of him.

Cassie was quiet all day. She'd gone out of her way to be the one to take care of the horses at our noon stop. And she'd sat quietly at the last station while we ate lunch. Sara was just as bad. She kept shooting Tim long-lost glares then looking away when he glanced back.

We dropped off the horses at the next station then continued on to the last where we stopped for lunch. Tim would be returning to his camp from this point on. We would be on our own.

When we finished, Tim turned and asked the station master how things were up north. The old guy shrugged and said, "No new reports. I sent along the last one about that group up just this side of Sandpoint. They said some guy named Bishop is setting himself up as the local warlord. But that was third-hand. So I don't know how accurate."

Tim nodded then glanced over at us. "I wouldn't worry, that was weeks ago." But I could see the doubt in his eyes.

I nodded. The closer we got the more worried I grew. Something was going to go bad. It had to. Life was too unfair. Especially now.

We returned and saddled the horses. Tim pulled his mount to the side, sighed heavily then stuck out his hand to me. "Tell Ryan and Chase not to take all the deer. We'll go hunting when I get back."

Sara stepped forward, "So you're not reenlisting?"

Tim studied her for a long moment then shook his. "I don't think so."

Sara seemed to relax as she smiled widely.

I could only roll my eyes and swing up onto Ajax then glanced over at Cassie. She was smiling sadly at Sara. God, what a tangled mess we all were.

Tim mounted, gave Sara a long last smile, then turned his horse for camp. We watched him for a second then hit the road headed north.

Sara was quiet and Cassie kept shooting me strange looks. Like she was expecting something from me.

Wow, this was so screwed up. I couldn't talk to her about it because my sister would go ballistic. But if I didn't talk to Cassie she was going to misread me and assume I was a jerk. And yes, I might be. But I didn't need her thinking that.

Chapter Twenty-Four

<u>Cassie</u>

I'll admit, I was confused. I mean, the whole world was screwed up. People were starving. Law and order had disappeared. We were on horseback. And my worst fear was wondering what Luke thought about our kiss.

I know, I know. I was being a silly girl. But come on, this was Luke Thompson.

My heart hurt just worrying about it.

I was still worrying over it when we were overtaken by five bikes. Young people about our age, all pedaling like mad. My jaw dropped. Of course, bikes had become the new transportation. At least for anyone without a horse.

They were faster than us walking. At least for now. But they'd tire out soon, I realized. I shuddered thinking about making the trip from Oklahoma on a bike. Leaning forward I patted Cimarron's neck, thanking him.

"What's the rush?" Luke called out to them.

The tail-end rider, a young girl about my age, a little overweight called over her shoulder, "There's a potato farm with an early harvest, they pay in potatoes. A tenth of all you pick."

Luke nodded. The girl hurried to catch her friends. I stared after her. Another sign of how things had changed. I swear. If you'd asked a teenager to ride a bike five miles so she could pick potatoes and she'd get paid in potatoes. She'd have looked at you like you'd lost your mind. I know I would have.

But now. Food. That drove everything.

We continued on, my gut tightening every time I saw Luke from the corner of my eye. What did he think? Why wouldn't he talk about that kiss? What did it mean? How was I supposed to act around him?

Then I would see Sara and cringe inside. She was going to hate me for the rest of her life. Sometimes it just sucks being a seventeen-year-old girl. What made it worse was the looks Luke gave me from the corner of his eye. Like I had terminal cancer and he didn't want to tell me.

Gritting my teeth, I ignored him until we stopped to make camp that night. He tried to help me set up the tent. I jerked it out of his hand and shot him my best death stare. He had the grace to back away, hands up.

The three of us sat around after a dinner of beef jerky stew and the last of our rice. The sun was dipping behind the mountains when Luke stood up, sniffing at the air.

"What?"

He pointed to a brown stain rising up from behind the ridge to the south. My gut fell when I caught a whiff of smoke. It wasn't the campfire. More sooty, more intense.

"How far?" I asked as I stood up next to him. Sara joined us to stare at the mountain.

He frowned then shrugged. "Close enough we need to keep an eye on it. Not close enough we have to move. Not yet."

Suddenly Sara's horse, Brandy, snuffed then stomped the ground. She'd obviously picked up the distant danger. Sara walked over to calm her down. She'd just reached the horse when Luke suddenly turned me towards him.

"I'm sorry," he hissed, obviously terrified about Sara seeing. Obviously talking about our kiss.

"I'm not," I hissed back at him as my anger grew. How could he be sorry about something so wonderful? And yes, I realize it was just me. But still, he'd started it. That kiss. This was all on him.

He took a deep breath then said, "I don't know what came over me."

The fear in his eyes made me want to laugh. This was all so stupid. We were running low on food, there was a forest fire a dozen miles to our south. The horses were nervous. And we were fighting about a kiss. Why?

Suddenly nothing seemed important anymore. My heart broke and I knew it would never mend. But my broken heart didn't mean a thing in this new world. "Don't worry about it," I said as I gently touched his arm. "It wasn't that big a deal."

I saw his shoulder slump in relief. The girl wasn't going to ruin his life about some silly kiss.

My heart broke even more but I kept my best smile on full blaze then turned to stir the fire and add a log. It was behind us. No big deal. Luke had kissed me. So? Plus Sara never learned about it so that whole hassle was avoided. No one was hurt.

Then why did my insides feel like mashed potatoes?

We returned to the fire. Sara had calmed the horses. I noticed that Clancy stuck close to Luke, picking up on our nervousness. We kept glancing up at the ridge until it got too dark to see.

I was about to go to the tent so I could wallow in my misery when we noticed orange lights dancing on the ridgetop.

"Crap," Luke cursed under his breath. The fire had topped the ridge and was racing down towards us. "Let's break camp. I don't want to get caught here if we get surrounded."

I swallowed hard as I saw the flames dance from one treetop to another. I'd lived in Idaho enough summers to know what a forest fire could do and how fast it could move. I didn't need any encouragement to get packed up and Cimarron saddled.

Fifteen minutes after getting the word and we were on the road. The air tasted of soot and the stars were blocked out by the smoke clouds. The only light was the distant flames. Luke kept us in the middle of the highway. Walking on asphalt was okay. Galloping, never. But it was so dark we might wander off into a ditch.

I fought the rising panic inside of me. Fought the need to spur my horse and get away. Rely on Luke, I kept telling myself. He'll know what to do.

We were making our way down through a forested canyon when Luke twisted in his saddle and pointed. Behind us and to the right.

My world took another turn to the bad side when I noticed the flames had jumped across the highway and were racing towards us on both sides of the road.

He then turned and pointed, off to the left the flames had gotten further along the top of the ridge. If they shot down too fast we'd be cut off.

"Come on," he yelled as he whipped Ajax.

I leaned over Cimarron's neck as I joined him on the gravelly shoulder. Sara took the other side.

The air was getting thick and I could feel my horse laboring to catch his breath. The flames had gotten bigger, closer, racing against us to cut us off. Jumping from tree to tree. Racing through the grass. Fighting to surround us and kill us. I swear, it was like an evil arch-villain. Every move we made the fire made a corresponding move to exterminate us.

My heart raced as I fought a terrified anger. We'd come so close. Almost made it to the farm only to have our lives snuffed out by this ... by this ... evil. It wasn't right. It wasn't fair. And the worst part about it all was dying without Luke knowing how I felt. Without him holding me and telling me he loved me.

God, I wanted that so much. I wanted to live.

Then I saw it. The flames had reached the edge of the road on the left. Luke raced over to join Sara then looked back to make sure I followed. Holding my breath I glanced to the left where the flames were temporarily held back by the road. And then to the right. The flames hadn't gotten to the road yet. A path. A small path was still open.

"GO, GO," Luke yelled as he spurred his horse and whipped him with his reins. Ajax balked, refusing to rush through the flames but Luke leaned forward and said something that got his horse to brave the approaching flames.

The other horses followed and we were through. A cinder burnt the back of my hand and the heat sucked the air out of my lungs. But we were through.

"Keep going," Luke yelled as he continued to race down the road's shoulder, constantly glancing behind us. Constantly worried the fire would catch us.

The horses were beginning to labor. They'd walked twenty-five miles that morning and had galloped for two miles through smoke-filled air. Plus they were scared out of their wits. I could feel Cimarron fighting to catch his breath and felt the foamy spittle from his mouth fly back and hit me.

"We need to rest," I yelled at Luke.

He pointed behind us then shook his head.

He was right, the fire continued to race down the Canyon. Suddenly Sara's horse stumbled. My insides clenched tight as I feared my friend being thrown from her horse at full gallop. That was how people ended up dead.

Sara squeezed with her knees to help steady Brandy and she regained her footing. Barely losing a stride.

We continued on for another mile, the fire constantly behind us. Suddenly, Luke Yelled, "There," and pointed to the left.

Enough moonlight broke through the smoke to shine off a small lake. Not much more than a large pond. Without another word, Luke pulled off onto a small trail and out into the lake. Both Sara and I followed. Out to where the lake tickled our horse's bellies.

Clancy came out far enough so that only his head was above the water. He'd take a few doggy paddles then return to get his feet on the bottom.

Cimarrons' chest pumped in tons of air and he fought to regain his breath. "Good Boy," I said as I patted his neck then turned to look at the approaching fire.

"Are we far enough?" Sara asked. Her voice tight with fear.

Luke took a deep breath then nodded. "The banks are covered in grass, they'll burn but there's nothing close enough to get us."

The three of us sat there, twenty yards into the lake, and watched the fire approach. Luke was right. It didn't make it all the way to the lake. Not the trees.

We watched as the flames engulfed each and every tree. Filling the air with smoke and yellow sparks rising up into the heavens.

My brain fought to hide the fear dancing through me. Why had we stopped? Why didn't we get away? My brain told me the truth. Luke was right. We couldn't outrace the fire. He'd taken us to the one place the fire couldn't get us.

But my soul demanded we flee. My lungs hurt with every breath. The horses shivered from the cold water. I could feel them wanting to race. Danger was to be avoided.

So instead, I forced myself to sit there and watch the awful display of Mother Nature at her worst. The sky was alight with orange flames. The lake surrounded. It became hard to breathe. A combination of racing heart and foul air.

Luke reached into his bag, then leaned down and dipped a T-shirt in the water before he tossed it to me. Sara saw what he did and followed his example as I tied the shirt around my nose and mouth.

It would keep the worst of the smoke out of my lungs. At least a small bit.

We continued to sit there when I caught Luke giving me a strange look. He caught me catching him then gave me that patented Luke smirk. The one that said, I'm cooler than a freezer. Nothing phases me. Don't you wish you could be as cool as me?

Before. That smirk would have made me angry. Pissed me off to the Nth degree. Nobody could be that calm. That cool. That confident. But now I could only laugh. Our kiss was nothing more than stupid, childish nonsense. We'd almost died. Again. But we hadn't. We were alive. And life was good.

Yes. Luke could smirk. We'd cheated death again.

God, I loved that boy. It could not be denied. A born hero. Handsome, sweet, brave. With a killer bad boy smirk. Every girl's dream. And yes he didn't care about me. Not the same way. And yes he was my best friend's brother. So there was a few problems with the situation.

But we'd kissed. I would always have that.

Chapter Twenty-Five

Luke

We sat there until the weak morning light. Twice during the night, I'd almost moved us back to the shore, it wasn't good for the horses, but a flare-up had stopped me. I didn't want to get caught. Not after we'd gotten away.

Swallowing my anger, I made us stay. Until we could see just how much damage had been done. My heart fell as the gray landscape came into view. Smoke still rose from smoldering tree stumps. Fallen trees interlocked, charred black.

The ground was covered in a gray ash. The air tasted like burnt toast.

The horses had been standing in water for way too long. They'd been sweating when we hit the lake. We would have to be careful or they'd all come down with pneumonia.

When we got back to the beach I made the girls dismount and take off the saddles so we could rub the horses down. Feed them oats and let them roll. They were soon covered in caked-on ash and mud. But they felt better.

We spent all of that day until the next morning by the lake until I was positive the horses would be fine. Of course, with nothing to do, I noticed Cassie shooting me strange looks. Hey, she'd said the kiss was no big deal. So obviously, I'd read too much into everything.

Hey, she was Sara's best friend. So it was better this way. Right?

Grumbling to myself, I grabbed my fishing rod and walked around the lake to a good spot, and spent the afternoon fishing. As I sat there, I could look across the water at Sara and Cassie and felt my guts tighten.

The fire had been too close. I'd screwed up. We should have hit the road as soon as I smelled that smoke. Long before those flames topped that ridge. But it had been a long day and I was worried about over-taxing the horses. My screw-up had hurt them way more than if we'd left earlier.

Thoughts about the mistake automatically had me thinking about kissing Cassie. I just couldn't get it out of my mind. It was such a dumb move. I'd made her feel uncomfortable. Risked pissing Sara off. All for what?

But still, I couldn't stop myself from remembering the way she had looked in that wet T-shirt when we got caught in the rain. Or forget about the way she felt in my arms. She fit perfectly. As if she'd been designed to slot into my arms like that.

You know that feeling when something is just right. Like hitting a baseball on the sweet spot. Sitting a bull and knowing you were going to make the eight seconds. Taking aim at a prize mule deer and knowing you were going to get him with one shot. Some things you just know are right.

But then I thought about Sara. Thought about Cassie's family. And the minor fact that she'd shown no interest in me. Not really. Hey, I'd had girls flirt with me. I knew the way they were. And I'll admit, there is nothing better than a pretty girl batting her eyelashes, twirling her hair, and laughing at your stupid jokes.

But Cassie wasn't like that. She was too smart. Too ... honest, to play stupid games. Besides, she wasn't interested, not really.

When I had enough fish for dinner and again for tomorrow's breakfast I returned to the camp. Cassie ignored me. Sara frowned. I pretended like nothing was going on and cleaned the fish.

The next morning we worked our way down the road into a long valley. The fire had flown down the canyon and then the valley until it reached a small town. Whipped through the town then carried on down the valley. It was like walking through a moonscape. Gray destruction everywhere.

My jaw dropped as we approached the burnt buildings. A charred mess of black ash and twisted metal.

The three of us stared. I tried to figure out if the building had been a businesses or a home. The bathtub sitting in a pile of charred planks. A home. Glass display cases, broken glass from the heat. A business. That was it. The only indications of a long history.

A town of about two thousand wiped out in one night. One more thing we had lost. Firefighters. Water pressure. Cars to escape.

People were poking through the debris, zombie-like, searching for anything worth keeping. My heart broke. This new world had already taken so much from them. Now this. All their food was gone. Burnt. Now nothing more than ashes blowing in the wind.

Their shelters were gone. They'd lost everything.

Looking around, I noticed clothes on the bank of a creek. No, not clothes, bodies. Three of them. One a small child.

The stares of bewilderment and pain in the survivors made me wince. How had they made it through the night? The bodies, what did they do wrong? The fire looked like it had raced through the town and continued on, devouring everything in the valley.

The creek? Like us, they'd found water. Had the people who died not made the water in time? Had it not been enough, had flaming trees from the bank gotten them?

We silently rode through town. No one asked us where we were going. No one tried to stop us. A middle-aged woman with salt and pepper hair had tear stains on an ash-covered face leaned on a charred rake. She stood and watched us with a cold, empty stare.

I wondered who she'd lost. And what would these people do come winter? It was something to remember. A fire could wipe out every bit of work you had done to prepare. An earthquake, tornado. So many things. There was no safety net anymore. One bad thing meant a long, slow death.

It took us half the day to break out from the carnage left by the fire. It looked like the wind had shifted and pushed the fire off to the north, up over a ridge then back in on itself.

The air still tasted of soot and I wondered if I'd ever get that smokey taste out of my mouth. I also kept thinking about the three bodies lying next to the creek, How many had died in the fire, unable to get away in time.

From the corner of my eye, I caught Cassie staring at me with a worried frown.

Get over it, I told myself. The girls did not need to see me worried or upset. It just made their lives harder. So I threw on my best - I don't care - look and pushed us to a camp just outside the Coeur D'Alene suburbs on some green grass.

We were pretty quiet that night around the campfire. Each lost in our own thoughts. I noticed Cassie glancing at me occasionally. Sara caught her and frowned. I ignored them both, unable to get the picture of the tear-stained woman out of my mind.

That could have been my mother. Suddenly I felt a wave of homesickness. Had we done the right thing? Leaving our home? Dad wouldn't have done it. He'd have stayed and fought.

But the girls were still alive. I know if we'd stayed they wouldn't be. I knew it deep in my soul. There were too many desperate people. All needing what we had.

As we worked our way through the city of Coeur D'Alene I noticed loose-fitting clothes. A lack of food. And everyone had to work for everything. I mean, how much walking were people doing? Washing clothes, dishes, searching for food. People were burning calories. Calories they didn't have.

More than one person looked at our horses with avarice. I ended up pulling my rifle and resting it across my lap. I noticed that both Sara and Cassie did the same thing and smiled to myself.

It took most of the day to get through the town. We passed a market but they didn't have anything we needed and I didn't want to stop. Further on, a man was selling meat from a stand. A large sign above his booth in large yellow letters said, "**One pound of Beef, ELK one ounce of gold.**" An old fashioned weighted scale sat at the edge of his booth.

He studied us, or really our horses, but I shifted my rifle and he had the good sense to stay behind his bench.

I noticed an army camp in a park and we paused for an afternoon meal next to their fence. I figured being close to them we'd be safe. An express rider came in from the north and raced off to the south. A boy no more than sixteen in army fatigues. I wondered if he'd been the boy to deliver Tim's letter to his mom.

Had that been ten days ago? God, it seemed like the world was moving so fast. Then other times it felt it was taking forever to get to Cassie's family.

I did catch Sara looking wistfully to the south.

That afternoon I pulled us off the main road and up a firebreak into the mountains.

Once we were in a couple hundred yards I jumped down and went back to wipe our tracks.

Both girls frowned at me, curious.

"We'll have a cold camp tonight. No fire. I didn't like the way those people were looking at us. If someone follows us. They won't find us up here."

The girls nodded. One of the many things I was proud about was their lack of complaining. My life could have been so much worse if they'd spent all day every day bitching.

No, not these girls. They were made of sterner stuff.

We spent a quiet evening gnawing on beef jerky. Once the sun had dipped down behind the distant mountains I grabbed my rifle and a blanket.

"Where are you going?" Cassie asked. Domanded really.

"There's a spot down a bit where I can keep an eye on our back trail."

She rolled her eyes then shook her head.

I patted my leg for Clancy to follow then left them there. I knew they'd be okay. I'd only be fifty yards away. They were both armed. And my gut told me I needed to worry about what was behind us.

Finding a tree with a clear path to see back down the fire break I sat down, resting my back against a tree. Clancy settled down next to me, facing our trail. The dog knew what we were doing.

Once it got too dark I'd be relying on him for a warning. There would be a moon tonight. The haze would knock down the light but there should be enough to see the trail and anyone approaching.

As I sat there I thought about our trip so far. How many times things had almost gone too wrong? Of course I also thought about Cassie. It seemed like that was all I could think about.

Suddenly, Clancy lifted his head. But instead of looking down the trail, he froze and stared back toward the camp. My gut tightened, had someone gotten between me and the girls.

I jacked a round into the rifle and was pushing up when Clancy suddenly started wagging his tail. Doing the dog dance of being happy to see someone.

Grumbling under my breath I said, "You can come out Cassie. I won't shoot you."

She stepped out of the darkness between two trees into the pale moonlight. My heart jumped. There is something about a pretty girl in tight jeans with the moonlight in her hair.

We stared at each other for a long moment then she said, "How did you know it was me and not Sara."

I laughed. "My sister has more brains than to sneak up on an armed guy in the middle of the night."

"It's not the middle of the night," she said as she held up a canteen. "You forgot this."

Chuckling to myself, I shook my head, accepted the canteen, then motioned for her to have a seat. She'd come all the way out here. I didn't have to send her back too fast. Besides. I'd enjoy the company for a bit.

She sat next to me then stared down the fire break. "Do you really think we will be followed?"

I shrugged, as I caught a hint of rose that tore my gut in two. How did she do that? Smell special? Out here in the middle of nowhere? I was going to ask but stopped myself. It was too personal. Instead, the two of us stared into the night.

A tenseness filled the air around us. An awkward silence that seemed to grow and grow every second it wasn't acknowledged.

I was trying to figure out what to say when she pulled her legs up and wrapped her arms around her knees before shivering. I didn't think, I just naturally removed my jacket and draped it over her shoulders before I put my arm around her and pulled her close to keep her warm.

She sighed and sank in next to me. Again, a perfect fit.

We sat there, neither willing to say anything. Staring into the dark. I was going to tell her it was time to go back when I realized she'd fallen asleep.

Leaning over, I pushed a wisp of hair behind her ear and settled back. Enjoying the feel of her in my arms.

This was how life was meant to be. Yes, tomorrow would be all screwed up and we'd go back to ignoring each other. But now, at this moment. Life was good.

God, how I wished it could have stayed that way.

Chapter Twenty-Six

Cassie

Okay, waking up in Luke's arms was special. Maybe the most special thing ever. I quickly wiped my mouth just in case I drooled all over myself then said, "You didn't sleep."

He shrugged as he continued to stare down our back trail. The sun was maybe an hour from coming up but we could see all the way down to the main road.

"Grab an hour," I told him. "I'll keep lookout."

He studied me for a moment then nodded. I swear, he was asleep within a minute. I would glance at him then back at the road but I couldn't not look at him. He was just so handsome. My heart ached with all I did not have.

An hour later he woke all by himself just as the sun crested the mountains to the east. He shook his head then shot me a quick smile. I sighed inside. I'd made his life a little bit better.

That became our life over the next few days as we passed by remote farms and chunks of clear-cut forest. The Idaho panhandle isn't known for being full of people. We'd move about twenty-five miles through the mountains. Up and down, around lakes, always on the main road.

At night we'd take turns keeping watch. Sara would take the first one, I'd relieve her around midnight, then Luke for the last four hours in the morning. I swear, the closer we got to my Papa's farm the scarier it became.

I was waiting for the world to end, - Again. Something had to go wrong. I just knew it.

Unfortunately, I was right.

We'd stopped for lunch just the other side of Sandpoint. A town of ten thousand. The last real town before we got to Papa's forty miles up the road. The horses were munching grass. I'd spread a blanket for a picnic. I was leaning back letting the sun warm my face when I heard an ominous click.

Slowly turning my head I saw three men stepping out of the forest, each with a rifle aimed at us. Luke cursed under his breath as he jumped up. Clancy growled deep in his throat at the threat.

"No you don't," the lead man said as he swung his rifle to cover Luke. My heart fell. How had we allowed ourselves to be so dumb? We'd let our guard down. One minute in months of being careful. That was all it took.

Our rifles were on our saddles. Luke's pistol was on his hip but the men had gotten the drop on us. I could see it in Luke's eyes, he was debating with himself whether to draw his gun or not.

"Don't," I said as I put my hand on his arm. Restraining him. The thought of him being killed made my heart slam to a stop.

He glared at me but he didn't fight me.

The men were all in their thirties. Dressed in camo like they were out hunting. And in a way, I guess they were. The leader was taller, with black hair and an evil glint in his eyes. The short one, a redhead, kept looking around like he expected to be attacked from a dozen different directions. And the third one, a bald, fat guy just stared at us with dead-eyed, soullessness.

"What do you want?" Luke demanded.

The leader scoffed then said, "Drop the gun, careful. It'd be a shame to shoot your girlfriends."

Luke sighed heavily but he slowly unbuckled his gun belt and gently lowered it onto the grass.

The three men seemed to relax but they kept their guns pointed at us. "Check it out," the leader said to the redhead as he nodded to our saddles and packs. The man scurried over and started rifling through our stuff. Finally, he said, "A week's worth of food,"

The leader smiled, "And four horses,"

"And two girls," the soulless fat guy said. My skin crawled as my heart sank. This was so not good.

The leader's eyes narrowed as he studied us. Obviously trying to figure out what to do next. Like a dog chasing a car. He'd never expected to actually catch us. But like I said, we let our guard down.

I glanced over at Luke and knew he was kicking himself. My heart went out to him. I knew him. He'd hate himself forever for letting this happen.

"My family won't be happy," I said. "They live just the other side of Elmira." Maybe if I could get them to think we were local. One of them. When that didn't work I tried for the sympathetic route. "We came all the way from Oklahoma."

He smiled, showing a dead tooth. "Bishop won't care."

My heart fell.

"Tie them up," he told his men.

Redhead handed his rifle to his partner then cut part off the rope on Luke's saddle and started to reach for Luke's hands. Clancy didn't like that and growled deep in his throat as he bared his teeth.

"Kill the dog," the leader said to the fat man.

My heart fell, "No." I yelled.

Fatman ignored me and started to swing his rifle. Luke growled as he swung and punched the redhead then turned and knocked the fat man's rifle just as it exploded.

Clancy yelped as he danced away.

"Go," Luke yelled at his dog as he wrestled with the rifle to keep it away. "Go now."

"Go," I yelled as I stomped at Clancy. One thing about that dog. He was probably the smartest dog in the world because he realized his only safety was the forest and he dove into the brush.

My heart soared when I realized there was no limp. No blood. He hadn't been hurt bad. Suddenly I heard a sickening thunk and turned to see the leader pounding Luke in the head with the but of his rifle as Luke wrestled with the fat man.

"No," I yelled as I raced at them, my fingers out like claws. I was going to rip this man's eyes out of his head. But the leader twisted and punched me in the face. A man's punch. Not a slap.

I fell like a bag of bricks, unable to believe it. In my entire life, no one had ever hit me. My father or brother or cousin would have killed them.

It was strange, painful, a dull thrumb echoed through my brain as I tried to understand what was happening. Then I saw Luke lying on the ground, blood leaking from the side of his head. His hair was matted by the red blood, making my insides clench.

Sara made a move to help her brother but was held back by Red Head.

My insides cringed with fear and shame. I had failed to save the man I loved.

He pushed himself up from the ground, his eyes glazed over in confusion, obviously fighting a concussion.

"That's enough," the leader yelled. "Tie them up. Like I said."

They tied Luke's hands behind him. They tied both Sara's and mine in front. I was confused until the fat man leaned close and whispered, "It's easier to lay you on your back this way."

My insides froze as I realized what he meant. No, this couldn't be happening.

"Saddle up. Bishop is going to love those horses."

"And the girls," the fat man added with a look that made my skin crawl like a thousand spiders were climbing up my arms. My soul cried with fear. This was so unfair. We were so close.

"You can't do this," Luke said.

The leader's forehead creased for a moment then he smiled just before he pulled back then punched Luke, knocking him to the ground.

I gasped, feeling the punch. Watching Luke crumble.

The leader scoffed then told his men to hold Luke. They grabbed him and held him while he proceeded to punch him in the stomach then the face twice more. I think he would have continued punching him but he hurt his hand, shaking it to rid it of the pain.

Luke's head slumped but when they let him go he didn't fall. Instead, he looked at Sara and me with swollen eyes, trying to send us a message. That was when I realized all their guns were on the ground or leaning against a tree.

Could I get to it before they stopped me?

Luke shook his head just a bit then stared off into the forest. Were we supposed to run? But how. They'd catch us. Bus Sara saw it too. She shot me a quick questioning look.

Turning, he watched the two men lifting the saddles. Just as fat man placed the saddle on Ajax's back, Luke whistled. Ajax reared knocking fat man into Redhead. Luke spun and kicked the leader in the groin then yelled, "Go, Go,"

I froze as the horses all began fussing and kicking out. Stomping, rearing. Both Redhead and Fatman fought to get them under control. The leader was down, groaning in pain. Luke knocked me. "Go, Go,"

I bounced out of my stupor and charged into the forest after Sara. We raced through the trees, dodging down and through. The pine needles that carpeted the forest floor muffled our steps.

We didn't follow a trail. If you've ever seen that part of Idaho you know what I mean. The trees are thick. With bushes and ferns between them. But Luke was like a rabbit, skimming by, ducking, and weaving until we were maybe a thousand yards up the hill.

My chest hurt as I gulped to get enough air. Luke stopped us behind a patch of boulders then turned and held out his wrists behind him, silently asking us to untie him.

Both Sara and I fought each other as we desperately tried to set him free while we gulped in air, fighting to stay alive.

She finally backed away to let me at him. I got him untiled then winced when he turned back to get my hands free. The man's face looked like last week's hamburger. Red and turning blue with blood leaking from three different spots.

Without thinking I reached up to touch his face.

He winced and pulled away.

My heart fell. He wouldn't let me comfort him.

Suddenly we heard a noise in the bushes behind us. No, they couldn't be that close. My heart stopped as we froze, too afraid to move.

Luke slowly bent and picked up a large rock then motioned for us to get behind him. We stood there waiting, fighting for breath, too tired to keep running. One man armed with a rock against three men with rifles.

Suddenly the bushes parted and Clancy grinned as he raced towards us. His tongue flopping from side to side. He quickly sniffed each of us, to make sure we were well then looked up at Luke, silently asking for his next command.

We each hugged the dog then Luke started us out again. "We need to get up the mountain."

"What about the horses?" Sara asked. "Our stuff."

Luke shook his head. "Getting away is more important."

I could see it in his eyes. He hated abandoning our stuff. Ajax, but he refused to risk Sara or me. I knew him. If it had been just him he'd have tried to retrieve the horses.

"He's right," I said. Partly because I believe it. But also to support him in the only way I could.

Luke sighed heavily then we heard the men calling out to each other down below us. My stomach fell as I realized these men would never stop.

"We need to find a place to hide," Luke whispered as he looked up the mountain.

I followed his stare then smiled. "I know just the spot," I told him.

Chapter Twenty-Seven

Northern Idaho

In a small town just north of Sandpoint, two men entered a restaurant. The cook pointed to the corner and said, "You can drop your gear there."

Ryan Conrad glanced over at his cousin Chase Conrad and shrugged his shoulders. Both young men lowered their backpacks in the corner. Ryan examined the place and relaxed. Two other men at a round table. The room was lit by an oil lamp and two candles.

"How much?" Ryan asked, nodding to the kitchen.

The cook said, "One bullet per meal. Two if they're .22s."

"We've got money," Ryan told the man.

The cook scoffed and said, "Folding money ain't good for nothing but the outhouse. And coins ain't real metal. Bullets."

Chase looked over at his cousin who shrugged. "I'm tired and don't want to cook if we don't have to."

Ryan shrugged as he pulled back a chair. He removed a .45 shell from his gun belt then watched as Chase did the same. They both placed their bullets on the table and looked at the cook. The man smiled as he poured them water from a pitcher, "Only got steak and mashed potatoes. And I only know how to cook the steak medium. And the potatoes ain't got butter."

Both men shrugged. They were hungry and just needed fuel. They'd walked almost thirty miles. It was the first day of a long trip and Ryan's leg wasn't fully healed. It felt good to sit down.

Ryan glanced over at the two other men and wondered about them but he kept his mouth shut. He was just too tired to care.

A few minutes later the cook came out with two plates, each containing a large T-bone steak and a double fist worth of potatoes. The cooked meat made his mouth water. He hurriedly cut into the steak but froze when he heard one of the other men tell his companion.

"A boy and two girls. Out of Oklahoma, they said. Bishop's men have them cornered, up on by the old Peabody mine."

The other man winched, "I wouldn't want to be them if Bishop gets ahold of them.

Ryan's heart dropped as he looked over at Chase. His cousin glared back then nodded. Both young men pushed back from the table and retrieved their packs.

"What about your dinner," the cook asked.

Ryan tightened his belly strap and shook his head. "You have it. We've got to go get my sister."

He and Chase started out the door when Ryan turned back to the two men sitting at the table. "You get word to this Bishop guy. If he or his men hurt my sister. I will ... we will hunt him down and roast him over a campfire for three days."

Both men blanched but then they saw that the young man was deadly serious and said, "We'll let him know."

Ryan nodded then joined Chase Conrad as they melted into the night.

Chapter Twenty-Eight

<u>Luke</u>

My face felt like a minced meat pie. Like a bull had stomped on me for a solid two weeks then come back for more. I had to squint out of one eye to see where I was going. The other eye was closed up tight.

We were in trouble. I'd screwed up and let someone take our stuff. Threaten the girls. And put us on the run in the middle of nowhere.

Gritting my teeth, I swore I'd get my revenge. But at the moment I needed to get the girls away. Cassie led the way, she said she knew somewhere we could hide. So we were following her lead. And I'll admit I might have to squint but that didn't stop me from staring at a cute butt in tight jeans walking uphill.

Sara caught me staring and punched me in the arm.

"What?" I barked.

She just rolled her eyes then pushed past me to join her friend.

Taking a deep breath, I tried to figure out what to do. I didn't have any weapons. I didn't even have a pocket knife to carve a spear. How was I going to get the girls away? Did I get them to Cassie's family then come back? I knew in the depth of my heart that I was going to get revenge or die trying.

Suddenly Cassie yelped then pointed at a wooden door set into the side of a hill covered in vines and bushes. I noticed a metal rail in the trail. Two of them but with a tree growing up between them.

A mine, I realized. An old one.

"Papa showed us one year. I came with him and the boys deer hunting. The first and last time. Papa said he worked in this mine when he came to Idaho. Got money to fix up the house. He wanted to show us for some reason. I think it was why he chose this part of Idaho to hunt instead of closer to home."

I bent as I fought to get enough air. That jerk had hit me in the solar plexus a couple of times and I was still trying to get my breath back. Twisting, I looked back and realized we hadn't left a trail. The soft pine needles didn't make tracks. Besides, something told me those three couldn't track an elephant in the snow. And you couldn't see the door unless you knew it was there.

It was chained shut but a large rock fixed that. I got the girls into the dark cavern then pulled the door shut, rearranging some vines, and prayed we could stay forgotten.

A weak light leaked in from the corners of the door. Sighing heavily, I leaned up against the rock wall and slowly slid down. The girls joined me. Sara pulled Clancy tight and buried her face in his neck fur.

Closing my eyes, I tried to ignore the pain and focus on the next step. My mind was off somewhere when Cassie leaned into me. I instinctively put my arm around her and pulled her close.

She must be terrified, I thought as I remembered those men and the things they'd hinted at.

We sat there for half of forever. Twice I thought I heard men outside, but it was just fear making my mind jump to the worst outcome. I thought about moving us deeper into the mine but I knew these old places were filled with holes and pits. One wrong step and you died.

It'd be different if we had flashlights. But we didn't even have a match or lighter, let alone a candle or lamp.

Instead, we sat about ten feet inside the front door at the edge of the weak light.

The light slowly faded as the day turned into night. Leaving us in the complete dark. This was different than dark outside. Out there, you had some light, stars, moon, something. In here it was darker than the inside of a woman's purse. Especially when one eye was already closed.

Cassie's stomach rumbled, reminding me that they hadn't eaten. My mouth was dry and my head hurt.

"What are we going to do?" Cassie asked.

"We sit here until they stop looking for us."

I couldn't see her but felt her sigh.

She was right, I thought, we couldn't sit here forever. We needed water, food, we needed to get to the farm.

The next morning a faint light began to seep around the edges of the door, reminding us that another day had begun.

"We need water," Sara said.

"There's a creek back about a hundred yards," I told her. "We can get some water then come back here."

Both girls frowned.

"Or ..."

"Or?" Cassie asked.

"Or I go get our stuff back."

Both Cassie and Sara froze then both said at the same time, "No."

I ignored them as a plan began to form in my mind. A long night leaning against a rock wall will make a guy think. These men were out searching for us. Probably individually, to cover more ground. Yes, it might work.

"You guys stay here," I said as I pushed myself up. My entire body screamed at me as every muscle yelled in protest, refusing to move without it hurting. But at least I could now see out of both eyes. Barely.

"What are you going to do?" Cassie asked.

Sighing, I turned to her. "I need you guys to stay here with Clancy. Too many people will make too much noise."

"What? No!"

"I'm not asking," I said, "I'm telling."

Both girls looked back at me like I was crazy but I ignored them and turned to leave, slipping through the door and closing it behind me before they could stop me.

"I'll be back in an hour," I whispered through the door.

It took me twenty minutes to find my first victim. I was darting from tree to tree, listening, watching, waiting. They had to be out here. Please, I begged, don't be together. Then I saw him, the redhead, coming up the trail. He was scanning the path for tracks. The idiot didn't know we'd avoided the trail.

This was going to be too easy. I grabbed a rather large log. About the size of two

302

baseball bats and hid behind a large Douglas fir.

I held my breath, waiting, terrified I'd be discovered. The man was armed and would kill me the minute he saw me. But he was an idiot. He was armed, I wasn't. He didn't need to worry. In his mind, this could end only one way.

Please, I begged myself over and over. Please. And I swear god answered all my prayers because the idiot was louder than a Mack truck. I readied myself and when he came around the tree, I swung.

I swung hard. Like I was trying to hit a home run.

It was my best cut ever. I caught him in the forehead and he went down. Dropped without a chance to call out. One moment he was walking up the path, the next he was out, flat on his back.

The log split into three pieces.

I hurriedly pulled his rifle, my rifle it turned out, away then used his knife to cut away his sleeves and tied him up then bound his mouth.

He was out hard and I wondered if he'd ever wake up. Really I didn't care. I studied him for a moment then unlaced his boots and pulled them off before tossing them in opposite directions. The ferns would hide them for a hundred years. He could walk home barefoot.

I felt whole again. I had my rifle, the man's knife. I had gone from prey to predator. I spent the next two hours searching for the other two men. I had to get them before they got others to help search.

It was tempting to go back and check on the girls. I sort of wanted to see Cassie's eyes when she saw me with a rifle again. I wanted to brag about taking out Mr. Redhead. But I forced myself to focus on my mission. The two others.

I wondered if I should just shoot them as soon as I spotted them. A shot would warn the other. So no, I'd sneak up on the second guy, whichever one I found first. But I could shoot the third guy.

Working my way along a creek I suddenly heard a horse whinny. Ajax, I was sure of it. He sounded just like that every time he expected an apple or carrot. It was his way of reminding me in case I forgot. More than once I'd had to go back to the house just to make sure he wasn't disappointed.

He'd sounded down the creek a bit. I bent over and started working my way down. When I cut across a firebreak I froze. Kneeling down I worked on calming my racing heart. Maybe they'd left someone behind to guard the horses.

I slipped back into the bushes and worked my way through the trees, keeping the firebreak to my left. Then I heard someone cough and then a man grunt in frustration and say, "Shut up."

My gut tightened as I slowly pulled a fern frond aside and peeked into a clearing. The horses were tied off to a rope between two trees. My heart suddenly fell. Cassie and Sara sat on a log, Bald Fatman stood behind them with his rifle pointing at them.

They weren't tied up and Sara held Clancy's collar.

No, this wasn't fair. They were supposed to be safe up in the mine. No. No. And I couldn't just shoot the guy, the rifle might go off killing one of the girls.

Cursing under my breath I hunkered down then felt my world end as cold steel was pressed to the back of my head. "Twitch, and you die," someone said.

My soul sank into nothingness. I'd failed miserably. Again. There was no doubt, this man would kill me, and if he did, the girls would be all alone. No, I wasn't going to die just yet. It would be wasted. I'd save it until it might do some good.

I slowly lifted my hand away from my rifle and stood up, lifting both hands into the air.

He shifted the gun from my head to between my shoulder blades and pushed.

I will never forget the look in Cassie's eyes when I stepped through the bushes into the clearing. It was a mixture of fear, disbelief, and worse of all, disappointment.

The man poked me in the back again and said, "I was just going to kill you. But I like the idea of you having to watch."

My stomach fell as I realized what he was saying. The idiot hadn't even removed my knife but I couldn't get both of them. Instead, I let my shoulders slump in defeat and tried to figure out a way to get them both together.

Of course, at that moment the man, the leader reached over and pulled the knife from its sheath. He frowned as he looked at it, twisting it back and forth, especially the bone handle with the brass but plate, then he glared at me. "Where's Jarrod?"

"Who?"

His glare intensified as he pulled his hand back to stab me in the gut. He was going to open me like a fish.

"Freeze," someone yelled.

I looked up as a new guy stepped out of the woods, his rifle pointed to Fatman's head.

Cassie gasped, "Ryan?"

The guy didn't look away from Fatman, just pushed the rifle against the guy's back.

My nemesis instantly shifted his rifle to cover me, "I'll kill him."

The new guy shrugged his shoulder then nodded over the leader's shoulder. We both turned to see another man step out of the forest, his rifle aimed at my attacker.

"Chase," Cassie called out. Her eyes in shock that quickly shifted over to the largest smile in the long history of smiles.

Her family, I realized as a relief filled me. The girls were not going to be raped. They weren't going to die.

Chapter Twenty-Nine

Cassie

"You're call," Chase said to the leader as he shrugged.

My world spun out of control. Not only was Luke in trouble, but my brother and cousin might get killed.

We were all watching the leader fighting to make a decision. Kill Luke, but get killed himself. Suddenly the Fatman twisted and tried to bring his rifle around. I felt my world ending. Everything was happening too fast.

He didn't make it. He didn't even get it halfway there when Ryan put a bullet through his heart.

He dropped, blood oozing out of the exit wound. The leader guy who was covering Luke saw they were serious and dropped his rifle.

Finally, something went right. Both Chase and Ryan looked at me and shook their heads. Ryan said, "Why are you always getting into trouble? I swear."

I frowned at him then jumped up to hug him, burying my head in his chest. Home, I was home. Everything that had happened since the asteroid hit. All of it slipped away as my big brother held me.

"Come on," Chase said nodding towards the horses. He never could stand anything emotional. "We need to get out of here before their friends show up."

"No," Luke said as he glared at the leader guy. "He punched Cassie. Threatened both of them. NO, he doesn't just get to walk away."

Chase studied him for a moment then shrugged. "I know why that pisses me off. If you'll move I'll shoot the bastard and we can go home.

"No," Luke said still staring at the man. "He's mine."

"Why you?"

I scoffed, "Because I'm in love with her." Then he swung, catching the man in the spleen. As if he knew the perfect spot, it hurt but the man wouldn't drop. Not yet.

"What" I mumbled.

Sara rolled her eyes at me, "Don't act all surprised."

I was about to argue with her as I tried to understand what Luke had said when the leader guy suddenly charged him. Luke stepped to the side then brought his fist down catching the man in the side of the head.

He dropped to his knees. Shaking his head, trying to clear the cobwebs. He looked up at Luke with pure hate then charged again. I swear, Luke was a master, he bobbed and weaved while he threw jab after jab. Never enough to knock the man out. Always just enough to inflict pain.

Within minutes the man was staggering, wiping blood from his eyes, desperate to get his hands on Luke. He was pitiful.

"Luke," I called out and shook my head.

He glanced over at me then let out a long breath and brought a big right fist up into the man's jaw. Something cracked as he rose off the ground. Only to crumple into a pile on the forest floor.

Luke stood over him for a moment, silently waiting for him to get up. But the man was out, probably for a long time. Luke looked up, catching my eye. Suddenly an awkwardness filled the air.

Had Luke really said he loved me? No that was impossible. But I might have heard it. How could I ask? No, I couldn't say, "Did you say you love me?"

So of course, my mouth did exactly that before I could stop myself. "Did you say you love me?"

He rolled his eyes then said, "Don't pretend you didn't know."

My jaw dropped as my world disappeared. There was only Luke. Without thinking I rushed across the clearing and threw myself into his arms. Being hugged by my big brother had been nice. Being hugged by Luke was perfect.

Looking down into my eyes he smiled and my heart melted. His face was a mishmash of cuts and bruises. But they were there because of me. I gingerly touched the cut lip and winced thinking about kissing him.

"Kiss her so we can go," Sara said.

Both Luke and I looked at her. She shrugged and said, "I knew I was going to lose this battle the third day after the asteroid hit. It just took you two way too long to figure it out."

I smiled at her then back at Luke. He smiled then leaned down and took my lips with his. Again, that was so Luke, nothing would ever stop him from doing what he wanted to do.

"Hey," Ryan said from behind me. Being the big brother I loved.

I pulled away from Luke and said, "You may be my brother. But his is my man. So get over it."

Chase laughed then clapped Luke on the back and said, "Let's go. You two love birds have a lifetime to figure it out. But we need to get you home."

We left the bodies there. If the leader guy woke up, good for him. If not, then tough. I rode behind Luke. Ryan took Cimarron. Chase rode Cochise bareback. We put ten miles behind us before it got too dark to see the road.

I spent that night wrapped up in Luke's arms. Unfortunately, Ryan and Chase were two feet away. But I knew in my heart we would be alone soon.

It was late the next afternoon when we turned onto Papa's road. The large gray boulder at the corner of his property brought back a hundred memories. Almost all of them good.

It hurt knowing he wouldn't be there to greet me. He wouldn't get to meet Luke. God, I wished Luke had known my Papa. They were so alike. The tough, silent type. The kind of men who got things done.

Luke had gotten us here, all the way from Oklahoma. We'd fulfilled our quest. We'd made it.

A dozen people came out to welcome us. Children, two older women. Haley squealed then handed a baby to a man and rushed to pull me down off Ajax. We hugged as we were introduced, Haley holding onto my arm the whole time, refusing to let me go as if she was terrified, I would disappear.

But she needn't worry. I was home. I was where I belonged. With the man I loved. With the man who loved me.

Epilogue

Sara

I was happy for Luke and Cassie. Really, I was. It's just that this new world sucked. I was reminded every day that I was alone. I mean everyone was paring up. Even the kids, Paul and Tania, were paired up. It was puppy love. But really, they weren't idiots. Who else was there in our world?

It wasn't only being alone. It was seventeen people crammed into one house. Chase and Meagan and her two brothers were talking about moving into the barn. We'd hung blankets in the living room to give some sense of privacy. But it still irked.

Yes, like I said, I was happy for Cassie and Luke. And yes, I knew the whole best friends and brothers rule had been broken. Shattered in fact. But I couldn't blame them. They were perfect for each other. She kept him centered. He made her feel special.

Like I said, Perfect. It was almost sickening.

Stepping out onto the porch, I looked at the farm. They'd planted three acres of corn. Another three of potatoes. They, no we, had five gardens with every vegetable known to man growing it seemed.

The boys were bringing back deer and elk almost every week.

We'd traded Cochise for a heifer and calf so we could have milk. We didn't need another horse. But milk and cheese were going to be important this winter.

That had become our focus. I'd been on the farm for two months and every day was prep for the winter. Farming, canning, drying, gathering berries or nuts, something. It hung over us like a sword.

And still, no matter how hard I worked I felt empty. As if something was missing. That made me laugh to myself. So much was missing. Prom, college, future husband, future career. Family. God, a sharp pain flashed through me when I thought about Mom and Dad. Would it always be there, this hollow pain? The emptiness.

I was staring into the distance when Cassie came out onto the porch and put her arm around me. I knew that she knew I wasn't right. But it couldn't be fixed. Not in this world.

Sighing, I said, "I thought I would take a jar of the blackberry jam over to the Devo's. I mean their son was so helpful. It's the least I could do. Besides, we need to know our neighbors."

Cassie raised a single eyebrow in question.

I was babbling. Obviously. But I also felt better. Having a plan. "Can you tell me how to get there? Brandy needs the exercise anyway."

Cassie laughed then said, "It's about a mile south. We passed it coming here. It's that big red barn. They've got a white split rail fence running along the road."

She continued to study me then said, "Do you want me to come with you."

"No," I said too quickly. But I didn't need her judging me the whole way. Besides, I sort of wanted to learn more about this Tim Devo. He'd seemed nice. And he'd said he might be coming home soon. Maybe his parents might know when.

Luke made me take a rifle and Clancy. I swear he was going to insist on coming but I cut him off. I was doing this alone. I refused to hide. Besides there hadn't been any trouble and it had been almost two months.

I stuffed the saddlebags with two jars of homemade blackberry jam and called for Clancy to join me.

My heart raced as I turned onto the main road. Would his parents figure out why I was there? To pump them for information about their son. Would they tell him?

What if he was already there? Suddenly my heart skipped with hope. No, I told myself. It was too early. The Army wouldn't let him go. Not yet.

When I saw the split rail fence I took a deep breath. The red barn was in the distance, a puff of smoke rose from the main house.

We turned off the main road onto the farm's dirt road. Clancy suddenly barked and raced up the road. I nudged Brandy to hurry. We weaved around a bend. I pulled Brandy to a hard stop. An older woman sat in the middle of the dirt, an older man's laying in the dirt, his head resting in her lap.

She looked up with tears streaming down her face. Her face was cut and bruised. A black lab lay next to her, trying to comfort her.

"Mrs. Devo?" I asked as I fought to understand.

She sniffed then said, "They killed my husband. Those Bishop men. They killed my Lance."

The pain in her voice tore my soul in two. She leaned over her husband, rocking his dead body back and forth.

My heart broke. How was I going to tell Tim about this? Suddenly I feared for him. I had only known him for a few days. But I knew what I saw. He was a young man who would tear apart all of northern Idaho to get Justice.

The End

Author's Afterword

I do hope you enjoyed the novel. My last series explored what happens when everyone dies, and technology is lost. This time, I wanted to explore what happens when Technology is lost resulting in everyone dying. Again, the important question, what would I do in that situation.

I have often wondered what would happen if my family was separated by great distance when the world ended?

As always, I wish to thank friends who have helped, authors Erin Scott, and Anya Monroe. And my special friend Sheryl Turner. But most of all I want to thank my wife Shelley for all she puts up with. It can be difficult being an author's spouse. We have a tendency to live in our own little worlds. Our minds drifting to strange new places, keeping us unaware of what is happening around us. Thankfully I am married to a woman who knows when to let me write and knows when to pull me back into the real world.

The first book in the series Impact (The End of Times 1) is available on Amazon. The next book in the series **"Justice (The End of Times 5)"** will soon be available on Amazon for pre-order. In the mean time, I have put in a small sample of the first book in my other series, The End of Everything (The End of

Everything 1) I truly believe you would enjoy it.

Thank you again.

Nate Johnson

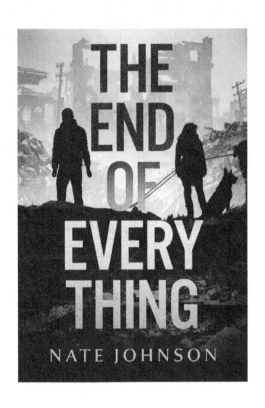

The End of Everything

Chapter One

Nick

I didn't say goodbye to my mom that day. A fact that I would regret on my deathbed. Being an angry seventeen-year-old was my only excuse. It was my mom who sent me away. Her way of stopping me from becoming an even worse jerk.

A boy gets in one fight and the world comes crashing down on him. Granted, breaking a guy's arm and knocking out a couple of teeth for the other one made it seem worse. But then they had it coming, believe me.

Anyway, Mom figured six weeks as a Counselor in Training at Camp Tecumseh in Eastern Pennsylvania would keep me away from bad influences. A nice peaceful summer, she said. God, how wrong could a person be?

But like I said, I didn't even turn to look at her when I stepped up onto the bus. If I'd known I'd never see her again, I might have given a damn. I might not have been such a jerk. At least I like to think so. It's how I keep from beating myself up about it.

I nodded to the driver. The same guy I remembered from my camp five years earlier. Then Dad died and going away to summer camp became an unnecessary expense. But Mom thought it would be good for me to do this CIT thing. It didn't cost anything. Free labor. So here I was on a bus to hell.

It was a day before the camp was supposed to start so this was just for the early birds. The kids and CITs that couldn't show up tomorrow. Nine kids and two girl CITs. Tomorrow there would be a hundred and forty campers arriving along with twenty CITs and staff.

Being the typical boy, I checked out the girls immediately. Both about my age, maybe sixteen. The one on the right had long brown hair in a ponytail. Pretty, with discerning eyes. Something told me, rich girl. I don't know. Maybe it was just the attitude.

The one on the left. Shorter, blond, with glasses. Pretty but not as much as ponytail.

I knew what they saw when they looked back at me. A tall guy with a scowl. I had a habit of standing out in a crowd. A fact that always bugged me at my core. I wasn't lanky. More solid. But tall. Six three and I wouldn't see eighteen for another two months.

The rest of the bus had nine kids, eleven to twelve years old, spread out. Five girls and four boys. They were looking at me with shaded frowns. Was I the typical jerk or a special one?

Shifting my backpack on my shoulder, I made my way down the aisle to the end then jerked my thumb for the kid in the back seat to move.

The kid had the good sense to scurry out of the seat.

I plopped down and stared into nothing.

The driver pushed the bus into gear, and we were off. Six weeks I thought. I could do anything for six weeks. It wasn't the end of the world.

Ha, that always makes me laugh. When it comes to being mistaken. No person had ever been more wrong.

The bus crawled through the small town and then started up a switch-back two-lane road into the mountains. I stared out the window at the forest and occasional farm of the Pocono Mountains. Not much different than the area around Syracuse, I thought.

Six weeks I reminded myself. I guess it was better than jail, even if only slightly.

A little over an hour and we finally got there, about twenty-five miles out from the town. I guess this place was farther out than I remembered. When you are a little kid, you don't pick up on things like that. But we were finally there, and things hadn't changed one bit.

About twenty cabins clustered on the far end of the lake. Four main buildings up on a hill above the lake and cabins. On the left, the admin building. Built of thick logs. Next, the combined mess hall and kitchen. Then the showers and restrooms. If I remembered correctly divided down the middle with six showers and eight cubicles on each side. It got busy in the morning, to say the least. And finally, the staff building. More like a dormitory.

Everything was as I remembered it. Even the same float sat in the middle of the lake.

I almost smiled to myself when I remembered the first time, I had swum all the way out there in a race with Billy Jenkins. I wondered where he was. Probably hanging out with his friends, playing video games, or a pick-up basketball game. Things I would end up never knowing. Billy was lost to history. As If he never lived.

I wonder if he'd been playing video games when it all ended. Fighting off monsters while invisible ones ate him up from the inside.

Three sailboats were moored to a pier sticking out into the lake, their sails furled and stowed. The large firepit off to the side looked like it was all ready for hotdogs and smores.

It was the first warm day of summer late spring day. A little cooler up here in the mountains with a high blue sky. But it was the smell though that told me I was somewhere different. A green smell filled with life. Or maybe it was the absence of car exhaust and wet asphalt. Anyway, I took a deep breath and almost relaxed. Then I remembered I was angry at the world and pushed it aside.

The blond and ponytail were waiting for me. The driver Thompson or Thomas or something was rounding up the kids and said he'd be back for us in a minute. The blond stepped forward with a wide smile and I knew the type immediately. She would want to be friends. For life even.

"I'm Brie Osborn," she said holding out her hand.

I shook it, making sure not to apply too much pressure. Mom had gone out of her way to try and make a gentleman out of me. For the most part, she had failed, but some things stuck.

"And this is Jenny," she said indicating the pony-haired girl.

"Jennifer," the girl corrected as she held out her hand.

Again, I made a point of not squeezing too hard. For the briefest moment we stared into each other's eyes, and I saw it immediately.

She didn't like me. To her, I was a bug that had dropped onto her plate of food.

I don't know what I'd done. And really, it didn't matter. She wouldn't be the first pretty girl who didn't think I was worth a damn.

Letting go of her hand, I turned away to look out over the camp. Six weeks, I reminded myself and then I was out of here. Two groups of snot-nosed kids to be shepherded.

As I stood there, an awkward silence fell over the three of us. I wanted to smile. They were pretty girls and weren't used to being ignored. But no way was I getting interested. Well, at least not officially.

Thankfully the awkward silence was broken by Thompson returning. He was the manager, I reminded myself. He'd been running this place for years. He had everything down to a system if I remembered correctly. A tight timetable that kept everyone too busy to get into trouble.

I wondered if he knew about me. There had been a police report. But the charges had been dropped when they finally figured out the two other guys were even worse jerks than me. No. He didn't I realized. He would never have accepted Mom's application.

Oh, well. No need to inform him of my past. I'd do my time then go home to finish out my senior year and then off to start some kind of life that I still hadn't figured out.

That memory. Standing there, thinking about the future hurts now. More than you will ever know.

Thompson returned after showing the kids their cabin. He had to be in his late forties with a bit of a paunch. A gray sweatshirt with Camp Tecumseh across the chest and a Yankee's ball cap that looked like it had been dunked in the lake a dozen times.

"Make sure they feel comfortable. Stop the arguments over who gets which bunk. You know stuff like that. Then have them up at the mess hall by five."

Jenny frowned at him. I had determined that I would refer to her as Jenny just to piss her off. "Aren't there any counselors? I thought we were supposed to be learning. You know the whole 'in training' part of things."

The old man had a brief worried look then shook his head. "A couple of them were supposed to show up today. But they got delayed. They'll be here tomorrow along with the rest."

Jenny decided not to push the issue but picked up her backpack and started down the hill. Obviously, she knew where she was going. If I had to guess, I bet she'd been a camper here for ten years and was going through this CIT stuff so she could get on staff next year.

As she walked down the hill, I had to admit her butt was way above average in jeans that were just the right amount of tight.

Thompson caught me checking her out and shook his head before slapping my shoulder. "Don't even think about it."

I laughed for the first time in two weeks. That was going to be an impossibility. I was a seventeen-year-old boy. That was all I thought about.

The blond, Brie, I reminded myself, hurried to catch up with her friend.

Old man Thompson showed me the boy's CIT cabin. On the opposite side of the camp from the girl's CIT cabin. With eighteen cabins for the campers between them. Obviously, these people weren't stupid.

I threw my stuff onto the farthest of eight bunks and wondered what the other CITs would be like. I shrugged my shoulders. I wasn't here to make lifetime friends.

Okay, it couldn't be avoided any longer. I found the cabin with the four boys and entered without knocking. You would have thought that a werewolf had stepped into the place. All four froze, looking at me with wide eyes.

I could see it instantly. Like all boys. At some point in their life they had been bullied by older, bigger boys. The natural instinct was to freeze in the presence of a predator.

Scanning them I saw the usual. Kids. The smallest in the back frowned, but I had to give him credit, he didn't look away.

"I'm Nick," I told them. "I'm supposed to make sure you guys don't get lost on the way to the mess hall. Any problems I need to solve? ... Good. Finish up."

They scrambled to make up their bunks. Sheets and blankets had been left on each one. Once that was done I had them put their stuff away in lockers. They still had that haunted look, waiting for things to go wrong.

"God, lighten up guys," I said. "I won't screw with you. Not unless you deserve it. What are your names?"

"Mike," a chunky kid with red hair said then bit his tongue, obviously wondering if that was the right answer. "Mike Jackson."

Okay. I know I can be intimidating. My size, the fresh scar over my left eyebrow. Oh yeah, and the permanent scowl.

"Carl, Carl Bender," a lanky black kid. Okay, if we had a basketball tournament, I was picking him for my team.

"Anthony, but I prefer Tony. Tony Gallo," A dark-haired Italian kid said as he pushed his glasses back up to the bridge of his nose.

I nodded then turned to the last one. The smallest, and probably youngest. "And you."

The kids finished putting his stuff away, hesitated, then said "Patterson Abercrombie."

The other boys laughed, and I saw the pain shoot behind the kid's eyes. I wondered how many times that had happened in his life and how many times it would in the future. Of course, we all ended up having way worse futures than people laughing at our names. But I didn't know that then so I did what anyone would have done and laughed along with everyone else, but I followed it up by saying, "That's too hard to remember. Besides, a name like that makes you sound like a stockbroker, and you look too intelligent to ever fall into that scam. So I'm going to call you … Bud. That okay?"

The kid's eyes grew big, and I knew he'd never had a nickname in his entire life. At least not one he liked. Smiling, he nodded.

"Okay," I said as I examined them. "Mike, Carl, Tony, and Bud. God, it sounds like a boy band. You guys break out singing and I'll disown you. I swear."

They laughed and the tension was broken. I wasn't a special jerk, perhaps only a regular one and they could live with that.

Oh, if we had but known what a person could live with and without.

Chapter Two

Jenifer

Camp Tecumseh, God, I loved it. The one place in the world that was safe. Safe from overprotective parents and a judgmental world. No maids reporting to mom every time I broke the slightest rule. I swear I think she paid them extra for every time they ratted me out. Here I could be me. Jennifer O'Brien.

The smells, the colors, the soft breeze. All of it brought back fond memories. And now, finally, I was a CIT. Everything was how it was supposed to be. CIT this summer. Then senior at school next year. After that, either Harvard or Yale. My parents were still arguing about which. But none of that mattered. I was at Camp Tecumseh for the next six weeks and my future was bright.

HA! What a crock of … stuff that turned out to be.

When we reached the CIT cabin I turned and looked back at that boy going into his cabin. Well, nothing could be perfect. All I could do was shake my head. This Nick person was so wrong for Camp Tecumseh.

I knew the type only too well. A bad boy to his very core. It was obvious, the heavy scowl, the wide shoulders, denim jacket, and the way he talked. As if everyone else in the world was without value. Yes, A definite bad boy.

Unlike most other girls. Bad boys did nothing for me. No fluttering butterflies. No halted breath. No, they were a waste with no socially redeeming value. Especially here.

Deep down, I knew the problem was that he reminded me of my dad. That same cocky attitude and that inability to be faithful. Mom might forgive my dad, but I still couldn't.

Brie glanced to where I was looking and smiled. "It is going to be an interesting summer."

I laughed and shook my head. "Let's hope not. Don't forget. We are here to keep the peace and make sure nothing bad happens."

Well, we failed at that, didn't we? Or at least the world did.

After Brie and I got settled we headed over to the girl's cabin. Brie and I had known each other for eight years. Not bosom buddies. But we'd shared a cabin a couple of times. Been on the same tug-a-war teams that type of thing.

When we got to the girl's cabin we knocked and waited to be let in. Five young girls. Three of them had been here before. The other two were newbies, watching the others to see what to do next.

I was pleased to see bunks being made and things put away in lockers. Eleven and twelve year old's. God, I remembered that awful time of being in between. No longer child, not yet woman. I smiled to myself. It was why girls this age formed such tight bonds with each other. They were the only ones who truly understood.

"I'm Jennifer, this is Brie. We're here if you need any help. Answer any questions."

The five girls stared back, some shrugging before returning to finish their work. I couldn't help but smile. Brie and I were already outsiders. We might be used for information, but we weren't one of them.

An hour on a bus and a shared cabin and they were already forming a team to face the world. After introductions, I watched them for a moment and immediately started putting them into categories.

Ashley Chan, Asian-American. A quick smile and a born helper. She was already assisting Katy Price in finishing with her bunk.

Katy Price, brunet, shy. When I saw her slip a Harry Potter book into her locker I had to smile. Only a true bookworm brings a book to camp. I knew she would have preferred to lay in the shade of a tree and read instead of swimming or games. No, for her, other worlds were her fascination.

Then there was Nicole Parsons. She was easy to figure out. A hint of eyeshadow and lip gloss. Twelve going on sixteen. With a hint of toughness behind her eyes. Nicole was the type of person you didn't want to get on the wrong side of.

Emma Davis, a strawberry blond was watching everyone else with a keen eye. A newbie, she had a natural curiosity. The diary sitting on top of her upper bunk confirmed it. She'd chronicle every detail. Locking onto paper what she couldn't remember.

And finally, Harper Reed. The other first-timer. Confident, not needing to watch the others to know what to do. Tall, pretty on her way to being beautiful. A future heartbreaker. Supermodel in training. A sketchbook slipped under her mattress exposed the secret to her soul. An artist. I wondered if she was any good. Yes, I thought. There was something about Harper that said she would be good at anything she did.

Five young girls. My responsibility. At least until the counselors showed up.

I shook my head. They really should have been here already, getting ready. I was disappointed in them. It was just plain wrong to treat Camp as unimportant. Of course, now it is hard to blame people for being late when they were in the process of dying. It seems sort of petty, if you know what I mean.

After getting everyone settled, we headed up to the mess hall for dinner. The seven of us went through the line for salad, garlic bread, and spaghetti. Not my favorite, but that was the thing about Camp food. You ate what they served, or you went without.

We all sat at a table off to the right. Talking, sharing, an occasional giggle. When the boys showed up, the feeling in the room changed. I couldn't help but shake my head. Even at this young age, the girls were very aware of boys being in the vicinity.

Of course the male members of our species were typical, loud, and rambunctious, with someone throwing a punch at another's shoulder. It was almost as if they were trying to draw attention to themselves. The four of them got their meals and made it a point of sitting as far away as possible.

They wanted attention but didn't want to get contaminated by girls.

Then there was that Nick person. God, what a cold, non-caring, waste of oxygen. He stepped up and Mrs. Smith, the cook, smiled at him as if he were special then gave him a double serving without him having to ask. And of course he skipped the salad entirely.

But it was when he sat down all alone, separate from the boys that I saw his true self. A loner. Most definitely not Camp Tecumseh material. Oh, well, it was only six weeks.

Again, HA!

The next morning was pretty much the same thing only pancakes instead of spaghetti. It had been a restless night. The newness was

338

already wearing off. The girls had probably stayed up half the night sharing stories about where they were from. Now it was simply a matter of waiting for the other campers to show up so we could get started.

I was trying to organize a volleyball game when Mr. Thompson and Mrs. Smith stepped out of the admin building and called, Brie, myself, and Nick over. The camp manager had a deep frown and kept looking to the front gate. Mrs. Smith simply shook her head.

My stomach clenched up just a bit. I knew that look. It was the look my father got when things didn't go the way he expected. It was just a matter of figuring out who to blame.

"There seems to be a problem," he said with a shake of his head.

The three of us stood there waiting. This could be anything from rat poison in the pancake batter to someone forgetting to order enough toilet paper.

I couldn't help but notice that the Nick person didn't frown. I swear the man could have been told he was to die in an hour, and he wouldn't have cared one way or the other.

"It seems," Mr. Thompson continued. "That some of the staff are still delayed. Mrs. Smith will have to drive the other bus."

It was a little confusing, how did he know they weren't arriving. I knew from long experience that there was no cell coverage up here. Then I suddenly realized that as a result of the changes he meant that there weren't going to be any adults left.

"You guys will have to keep an eye on things."

Okay, I could live with that. A bit better than rat poison.

"Nick, you'll be in charge. Keep them away from the lake and the forest. It will only be a couple of hours."

Mr. Bad boy nodded, as if it was no big deal, being left in charge. I of course wanted to scream, how come he got picked? But I had learned long ago not to challenge older men. It was a waste of time, they never saw reason. My father being a prime example.

"There is stuff to make sandwiches," Mrs. Smith said, "If we're not back in time for lunch. But no using the stove and stay out of the ice cream. That is for special circumstances."

That last line makes me want to both laugh and cry. I'll tell you about it when we get to that part of the story.

Mr. Thompson stared at the front gate for a minute and shook his head Then took a deep breath and nodded for Mrs. Smith to follow him.

We three CITs were joined by the nine campers and stood there to watch the two big yellow buses drive through the front gate.

I think that is the point where my story started. Really. There was my life before and my life after. A life in what used to be the normal world and this life. Believe me, they aren't the same. Not even close.

The End of Everything (The End of Everything 1)

Made in the USA
Coppell, TX
26 November 2024